ACCLAIM FOR ANDREW KLAVAN

"I'm buying everything Klavan is selling, from the excellent first-person narrative, to the gut-punching action; to the perfect doses of humor and wit . . . it's all working for me."

—JAKE CHISM, FICTIONADDICT.COM

"Through it all, Charlie teaches lessons in Christian decency and patriotism, not by talking about those things, or even thinking about them much, but through practicing them . . . Well done, Andrew Klavan."

—THE AMERICAN CULTURE

"This is Young Adult fiction . . . but the unadulterated intelligence of a superb suspense novelist is very much in evidence throughout."

—BOOKS & CULTURE

NIGHTMARE CITY

ALSO BY ANDREW KLAVAN

The MindWar Trilogy

MindWar

If We Survive
Crazy Dangerous

The Homelanders Series

The Last Thing I Remember
The Long Way Home
The Truth of the Matter
The Final Hour

NIGHTMARE CITY

ANDREW KLAVAN

THOMAS NELSON
Since 1798

NASHVILLE MEXICO CITY RIO DE JANEIRO

Published in Nashville, Tennessee, by Thomas Nelson. Thomas Nelson is a registered trademark of HarperCollins Christian Publishing, Inc.

Thomas Nelson, Inc., titles may be purchased in bulk for educational, business, fund-raising, or sales promotional use. For information, please e-mail SpecialMarkets@ThomasNelson.com.

Publisher's Note: This novel is a work of fiction. Names, characters, places, and incidents are either products of the author's imagination or are used fictitiously. All characters are fictional, and any similarity to people living or dead is purely coincidental.

ISBN: 978-1-59554-798-9 (TP)

Library of Congress Cataloging-in-Publication Data

Klavan, Andrew.
  Nightmare City / Andrew Klavan.
    pages cm
  ISBN 978-1-59554-797-2
  I. Klavan, Andrew. II. Title.
  PS3561.L334N54 2013
  813'.54—dc23   2013023670

Printed in the United States of America

14 15 16 17 18 RRD 6 5 4 3 2 1

A12006 434599

This book is for the Ditmore Family—Michael, Rebecca, Nick, Catie, Morgan, and Jessie

PART I

THE HORROR IN THE FOG

1.

om was in heaven when the phone rang. At least, he thought it was heaven. He had never been there before, and the look of the place surprised him. It wasn't what he was expecting at all.

Then again Tom had never really thought about heaven much. When he had, he'd pictured it as a place in the sky where dead people with newly issued angel wings sat on clouds and—whatever—played the harp or something. This, though—this heaven he was in now—this was just a sort of park, an expansive lawn with walkways curving through it and fountains spouting here and there and vast, majestic temple-like buildings with marble columns and peaked facades. There were no clouds to sit on. There were no clouds at all. A sky of perfect, unbroken blue covered and surrounded everything.

As for the people—the people strolling on the paths or sitting on the benches or standing amid the columns of the temples—they were also not what Tom expected. No wings for one thing. No harps either. Just ordinary men and women in all the various shapes and colors people come in. Dressed not in spotless robes but in casual clothes, slacks and skirts, shirts and blouses. And when Tom looked at them more closely, they didn't seem as happy or as serene as he would have expected people in heaven to look. Some looked downright lost or fretful, worried or even sad. One man in particular caught Tom's eye: a lanky young guy in his twenties or so with long, dirty blond hair and a thin, hungry-looking face; sunken cheeks and darkly ringed eyes. He was standing in front of one of the Greek temples, turning nervously this way and that as if he didn't know where he was or how to get home.

Tom's curiosity began to kick in—that eager electric pulse that compelled him to know more, to search for the truth, to solve the puzzle. He could never resist it. Even though he only worked for a high school paper, he was a real reporter nevertheless. It was his nature. It was who he was. Whenever there was a mystery, he didn't just want to solve it, he *needed* to. And this was a mystery: What sort of heaven included fear and loneliness?

He had to find someone who could give him some answers—and it suddenly occurred to him that, since this was heaven, he knew just the person to look for.

He took a step forward toward the park—and then the phone began to ring.

And suddenly, heaven was gone.

2.

Tom opened his eyes and he was in his bed at home. A dream. Heaven was a dream. Well, *yeah*. What else was it going to be? It wasn't like he was dead or anything.

The phone rang again—his cell, playing the opening guitar riff from the classic Merle Haggard song "The Fightin' Side of Me." Dazed, Tom followed the sound to find the phone. It was on his computer table, jumping and rattling around as it rang. He reached out and grabbed it, looked at it to see who was calling. *Number blocked*, said the words on the readout screen. Which meant it was probably Lisa McKay, his editor at the *Sentinel*. *What time is it, anyway?* he wondered. What did she want from him this early on a Saturday morning?

Tom answered. "Yeah."

The phone crackled against his ear. Static—loud static—a wash of white sound, like the sound of the ocean in a seashell. Something about that noise raised goose bumps on Tom's arm, though he couldn't have said exactly why. It was just that the static sounded strangely far away. It echoed, as if it were coming to him up out of a deep well. It made Tom feel as if he were listening to a noise from a foreign, alien place, another planet or something like that. Weird.

"Hello?" he said more loudly.

Nothing. No answer. Just that weird, white, alien noise. And then—wait—there *was* something. There was someone on the line. A voice—a woman's voice—talking beneath the rattle and hiss.

"I need to talk to you. It's very important . . ."

The words, like the static, seemed to come to him from across a great distance. Tom just barely caught those two phrases. After that the words were unintelligible. But the woman was still talking and her tone was insistent, urgent, as if she was desperate to be heard.

"Hello? You've got a bad connection," said Tom loudly. "You're breaking up. I can't hear you."

The woman on the other end tried again. She wasn't shouting or anything, just talking in a very firm, insistent tone, trying to get through to him. Tom listened intently. He thought he recognized her voice, but he couldn't quite place it. He thought he heard the word *please*. He thought he heard the phrase "You have to . . ." But aside from that, the words were washed away by that ceaseless, distant, echoing static. It was frustrating.

"I can't hear you . . . ," Tom began to say again—but then it stopped. All of it stopped. The voice. The static. It was all gone and the phone was silent. There were a couple of beeps on the line. Tom lowered the phone from his ear and checked the readout: *Connection lost*.

For a minute he tried to figure out who it had been, whose voice he had heard. It was so familiar. He had been this close to recognizing her . . . But no, he just couldn't get it.

He shrugged and put the phone back on the computer table. Whoever it was, she'd call back, for sure. She sounded like she really wanted to talk to him.

Tom sat up in bed, tossing the comforter aside. He shook his head to clear it. Weird call. Weird noise. Woke him up out of that great dream, too. What was it? Oh yeah, he remembered: heaven. He sat there, looking around at the room. It was funny, he actually felt a little disappointed to be back from his dream, to be here again. It had been a nice dream, a restful place. And now the memories of it were breaking up in his mind, the images trailing away like smoke in the wind. He could barely remember what it had been like, and he was sorry to see it go.

He got up. Went to the dresser, started pulling out some clothes, dropping himself into them: sweatpants and a Tigers sweatshirt. He figured he'd go for a run after breakfast, maybe hit the gym at the Y.

His room was small. The bed, the dresser, and the worktable were all crowded together. Just about every space on the blue wall was covered with some picture or decoration or something. There was his unusually long American flag. His pennant for the Tigers, the school's football team. Another pennant for the Los Angeles Dodgers, even though, let's be honest, they were going to stink this year. There was a picture of his brother, Burt, looking all brave and noble and cool in his army uniform. And a bulletin board with some snapshots of Tom and his mom and Burt and some of Tom's friends. Then there were a couple of framed copies of the *Sentinel*. There was the issue that had his first front-page story on it: "Governor Visits Springland High." And there was another—the one with the big story—the biggest story and the one that started all the trouble for him. The banner headline was huge: "Sources: Tiger Champs Used Drugs."

Tom left his bedroom and went down the hall to the bathroom—but he paused for a moment at the top of the stairway. He stood listening. His mom's bedroom door was open and he could see her room was empty, her bed all made up. But he didn't hear her moving around downstairs. That was kind of odd, actually. It was after eight. Normally this time of the morning on a weekend, Mom would be rattling around the kitchen or vacuuming, doing the housework she didn't have time to do during the week. But the house was totally quiet below. Not a noise to be heard.

Tom continued into the bathroom, trying to explain the odd silence to himself. Maybe they'd run out of eggs and Mom had ducked out to the store for a minute to do the shopping. Or maybe she'd gotten up late and was just going down to the bottom of the driveway to get the newspaper.

Whatever. He washed up and shaved and stopped thinking about it. He was wondering instead if the Dodgers had won last night—for a change—and trying to remember who the starting pitcher had been.

He toweled the shaving cream off his face and took a look at himself in the mirror. He didn't like his looks much. He didn't think his face looked brave or noble or cool like his brother Burt's face. But then maybe, like a lot of people, he couldn't see himself as others saw him. The fact was, when he used his fingers to brush his black hair back, his blue eyes shone out intense, smart, steely and unwavering. His features were narrow and sharp, serious and purposeful. He didn't see it himself—he couldn't see it—but anyone else who looked at him recognized a young man who knew how to go after what he wanted, a young man who could not easily be turned away.

He came out of the bathroom, went downstairs, thumping half the way down, creating the satisfying thunder of a buffalo stampede, then leaping the rest of the way, his hands on the banisters, his sneakers hitting the floor so hard when he landed that the light fixture in the foyer ceiling rattled. Now he was sure his mom wasn't here, because normally when he came down the stairs like that, she'd call out to him with some snarky remark like, "Hark, I hear the pitter-patter of little feet." Or something. But there was nothing. No noise in the house at all. Just silence.

He glanced out through the sidelight next to the front door, looking past the gold star decoration on the glass. *Well, that's weird*, he thought. A puzzle. His mom's Civic was in the driveway. So she hadn't gone to the store. So where was she?

Tom was about to turn away when his sharp eye noticed something else, too. The newspaper was there, outside, lying at the end of the driveway where the delivery guy had tossed it. That really *was* strange. His mom was the only one in the house who read the paper. Tom got the sports scores off his phone and checked the rest of the news online. But his mom—the first thing she did every morning—the second she came downstairs, before she started making breakfast, before she did anything—was bring in the paper so she could read it while she drank her coffee.

So yeah—a puzzle: Where was she?

"Mom?" he called.

Just the silence in answer. And it was that kind of silence that goes down deep. It made Tom feel sure that the house was empty.

He opened the door and stepped out. He went down the driveway, the gravel crunching under his feet. Bent down to pick up the paper. Straightened—and again, he paused. And again, it was strange . . . Like, really strange.

Tom lived in Springland, California. It was a small beach town north of L.A. Usually the weather was just about perfect here—clear skies, sixty-five degrees in winter, eighty in summer, seventy in between. Today, though—though it was late April—it was cold and damp. The marine layer—the fog—had come in off the water, and come in thick. To his right, Tom could see past the Colliers' driveway next door, and after that there was nothing but a wall of drifting white mist. Same to his left: he could see the Roths' driveway and the Browns' across the street—and then nothing but fog, slowly swirling in the early morning breeze.

But that's not what was so strange. The fog was like that sometimes here. It would totally shroud the place in the morning, then burn off by noon and give way to a clear, warm Southern California day. No, it wasn't the fog that made Tom pause.

It was the silence. Deep silence. Just like in the house. It made Tom feel like the entire neighborhood was empty. Which was crazy.

Alert, that pulse of curiosity beginning to rise in him, he turned his head slowly from side to side, looking, listening. Something was missing here. What was it?

It came to him. Birds. There were no birds singing. No birds singing on an April morning. What was that about? Must've just been some sort of coincidence, all the birds stopping at once, a bird coffee break or something, but then . . . where was the noise from the freeway? The freeway wasn't even a quarter of a mile away. Normally Tom didn't hear it because he was so used to the constant *whoosh* of traffic that it just sort of faded into the background of his mind. But it was always audible. He could always hear it if he listened. And yet, he was listening now—and he didn't hear it at all.

Something new rose beneath his curiosity: fear. Not a

lot of fear: he was sure there was a reasonable explanation for all this. But a definite chill went through him, a finger of ice reaching up out of his inner darkness and touching him on the spine. No bird noise? No freeway noise? And no one on the street? What was this? Normally there'd be someone around. Stand here long enough and you'd see Mrs. Roth walking her dog or Mr. Collier taking out last night's garbage. A car driving past. Or old lady Brown—Mrs. Brown's mom, who lived with the Browns—looking out at him from the window in the gable upstairs. That was pretty much all she did all day: look out her upstairs window at the neighborhood, at anyone who was passing. But the gable window was dark. There was no one there. There was no one anywhere as far as Tom could see.

Still feeling that little chill of fear, Tom turned again and looked into the thick fog. A thought went through his head. It was a really unpleasant thought. He suddenly had the idea that something was moving in there, moving unseen in the depths of the mist. He had the idea that whatever it was—whatever was moving in the fog—was coming toward him, shuffling slowly toward him so that any minute now it would break out of the swirling whiteness and he would see it . . .

Tom gave a snort of a laugh. Imagination kicking into overdrive, that's all it was. "Silliness," as his mother would call it. And in this case, she'd be right. He was creeping himself out with silly thoughts. His reporter's mind looking for a puzzle where there was none. The marine layer was thick this morning, that's all. The fog muffled the noise—bird noise, freeway noise, all the noise. And as for the rest, it was a quiet street. It was Saturday. People were sleeping in. There was nothing strange about any of it.

You're being kind of an idiot, Tom told himself.

He started back up the path with the paper in his hand.

So where was his mother, then? The question niggled at him. He could never let a question go until he had the answer. Still, he tried to shake it off.

She was probably abducted by aliens, he told himself. *That has to be the most reasonable explanation, right? Either that or she took a walk. But nah, I'm going with aliens. That's gotta be it.*

Tom was smiling to himself—smiling at himself—as he stepped back into the house. Smiling, he shut the door behind him. Smiling, he tossed the newspaper onto the front hall table: *whap.*

Then he stopped smiling.

He heard something. He heard a voice. It wasn't his mother. It was a man talking. It was coming from inside the house.

Tom was still a little spooked by the idea that had come

to him outside—the idea that there had been something moving around in the fog. His heart beat a little quicker as he walked down the hall toward the sound of the voice. With every step he took, the voice grew louder, more distinct. He started to be able to make out some of the words the man was saying.

"... your mission ... what you have to do ... remember ..."

Tom came to the end of the hall and stepped into the kitchen. That sharp eye of his—and that sharp, questioning mind—saw immediately that his mom hadn't been in here this morning. She hadn't been in here at all. The lights were out. There were no dishes in the sink. There was nothing cooking on the stove. No trace of food on the counter. The place looked as it always did after Mom cleaned it for the last time at night and before she used it first thing in the morning.

Where is she?

Then he noticed something else. The voice—the man's voice—was coming from the basement.

"... the game is the point ... play the bigger game ...," the man was saying in a firm, even tone. Then there was something Tom couldn't make out because the basement door in the kitchen was closed and the voice was muffled. Then he heard, "... that's the mission ..."

Tom hadn't realized he'd been holding his breath, but it came out of him now. Everything suddenly fell into place with satisfying certainty. Tom and his brother, Burt, had fixed half the basement up into a family room two summers ago. Most Southern California houses didn't have a basement at all, so they'd wanted to take full advantage of theirs. They'd paneled the walls and laid carpet down over the stone floors. They'd set up an entertainment center complete with a flatscreen, a couple of humongous speakers, two game consoles, and a laptop control center—some of which Tom had paid for himself with money he made that summer busing tables at California Pizza Kitchen. They'd even put in a small refrigerator so they wouldn't have to run up and down the stairs for sodas and snacks in the middle of a football game or a *Call of Duty* shoot-out.

Mom didn't go down into the basement much except to do the laundry in the other half of the space. She said she couldn't even figure out how to turn the TV on. But that was a typically Mom-like exaggeration. She could turn it on when she wanted to. So, obviously, that was the answer. Obviously she'd gone down to the basement this morning and was watching TV for some reason. Maybe there was a big news story breaking and she wanted to find out about it before she made breakfast.

Tom stepped into the kitchen, pulled open the basement door—and froze stock-still, his heart pounding hard in his chest.

"This is what you have to do," said the voice from the basement, quiet but firm. "Do you hear me? This is the point of everything. There's no getting around this."

Tom's mouth went dry, his satisfying certainty gone as quickly as it had come. That was not the television. He could hear the man clearly now and he recognized the voice right away. He'd have known that voice anywhere. It was Burt's voice. It was his brother.

Now Tom was scared again, and not just a little scared this time. This time he was *really* scared.

Because his brother, Burt, went on talking quietly in the basement. And his brother, Burt, had been dead these six months past.

3.

As Tom started down the stairs, his mind was searching for answers again. His brother's voice must be coming from a video—sure, that's what it was—some old vid of Burt that Mom was watching. That made sense. Mom was sad about Burt getting shot in Afghanistan. They were both sad—incredibly sad—how could they not be? Burt had been the coolest guy in the universe. Brave, honest, humble, funny. He'd been there for Mom whenever she needed him. He'd been Tom's best friend and his guide through life. So yeah, they were sad. And so Mom, feeling sad, had gone downstairs and pulled up one of their old video files of Burt so she could see his face again, hear his voice.

That's why she hadn't picked up the paper. That's why she wasn't making breakfast or vacuuming or whatever. She was down in the basement, feeling sad and watching a vid of Burt. That made perfect sense.

It did make sense—but Tom knew it wasn't true. In the months since Burt had been killed by a Taliban sniper, he himself had watched every video they had of him. Burt clowning around. Burt teasing Mom. Burt wrestling with him and so on. There was nothing on any of those videos like what he was hearing now: Burt's voice barking out with so much intensity, so much urgency.

"This is your mission, do you understand me?!"

Like he was talking to his fellow soldiers. Like he was giving them a pep talk before they set out into the wilds of the Hindu Kush. They had no video of Burt like that.

Tom licked his dry lips. He flicked the light switch on the wall. The basement lights went on below him. He couldn't see much down there—just a little section of stone floor at the foot of the stairs. You had to turn the corner before you came into the family room where all the equipment was.

Anything could be waiting around that corner, he thought.

But then he forced himself to stop thinking that. *Don't wimp out on me, Harding.* What could be down there? This wasn't a horror movie. This was real life.

He continued down the stairs. He told himself again that he was being an idiot for feeling afraid. Whatever the reasonable explanation was, there had to be one. Just because he couldn't think of it, didn't mean it wasn't there.

And yet, it was so strange, *so* strange. With every step he took, Burt's voice grew louder, clearer, more unmistakably Burt's . . .

"Look, what did you think this was? A joke? It's not, man! It was never that. Remember the Warrior. Right?"

. . . and yet, it couldn't be a video because they had no video like that. And it couldn't be Burt.

Because Burt was dead.

Tom had to force himself to breathe as he continued down into the cellar, step by slow step.

"This is what you have to understand," said Burt from the family room. "This is what I've got to get you to understand."

Just as Tom reached the bottom of the stairs, just as his sneaker touched down on the basement floor, Burt's voice suddenly stopped in mid-sentence.

"This is exactly what I was always trying to get you ready to . . ."

And silence.

Tom halted where he was. He swallowed hard. The silence went on for a single second. Then:

"Dr. Cooper to the ER—stat!"

A totally new voice! A woman's voice. Speaking as if over a loudspeaker. And then a man was shouting, "Single GSW to the chest! Clear Trauma One!"

Tom narrowed his eyes in confusion. He recognized these voices, too. They belonged to the actors on his mom's favorite doctor show, *The Cooper Practice*. It was a show about a bunch of doctors in a hospital who spent their days falling in and out of love with one another between treating emergencies. Real realistic—in the sense of being not realistic at all. But Mom liked it, so Tom had watched it with her a couple of times.

"How's his pulse?" one TV actor shouted to another.

"Sixty and falling fast," another actor shouted back.

So that was it. Mom was down here watching her favorite show on TV. Big mystery solved, right? Tom was already beginning to think he had only imagined hearing Burt's voice a second ago. He turned the corner and stepped into the family room.

"Mom?"

But the room was empty. Mom wasn't there.

There was nothing there but the entertainment center. The armchairs arrayed on the carpet around the flatscreen were empty. The TV was turned away from him so he couldn't see the screen, but the shouts were definitely coming from the set. And they were definitely from the doctor show.

"Where's Dr. Cooper?"

"We don't have time to wait for him. Let's go! Let's go!"

Tom glanced through the door into the laundry room, just in case Mom was listening to her show while she loaded the washing machine. But no Mom there either. And the washing machine and dryer were both off, both silent.

Tom moved around the brightly lit family room until he could see the front of the TV. There on the screen, sure enough, was the doctor show in progress. It was the usual sort of scene: a bunch of doctors and nurses and aides crowded frantically around a gurney as they rolled it into the emergency room. Everybody shouting about a GSW—which meant a gunshot wound, as Tom knew from a *Sentinel* story he'd written about the Springland police. Tom couldn't see the patient on the gurney, but he was sure it was someone on the brink of death. Patients were always on the brink of death on *The Cooper Practice*. Nothing new about that. Nothing strange at all.

But where had Mom gone off to after she turned the TV on?

Tom found the remote lying on one of the chairs. He picked it up and clicked the TV off.

"Mom?" he shouted.

But no—no answer here either. There was just the same silence as there was upstairs: that silence that made him feel the place was empty.

All right, he thought. *Enough of this stupidity. Let's find out what's going on. Right now.*

Tom jogged upstairs, taking the steps two at a time, pausing only to hit the light switch at the top. (*Electricity costs money*, he could practically hear his mom say.)

He swung round the corner. Jogged down the hall. Up the stairs again. Back into his bedroom. He retrieved his cell phone from where it was still lying on the worktable. He hit the button to call up his speed-dial list.

"What?" Tom whispered aloud into the silent house.

The speed-dial list was empty.

All right. Must've accidentally erased the list. Or something. No big deal. He went into his contacts list.

Again Tom spoke out loud, more than a whisper this time: "What. Is. Going. On?"

His contacts list had been completely erased as well.

For a second, Tom actually considered the possibility he was still dreaming. Sure, why not? You see stuff like that in the movies, right? Guy has a scary dream, sees a monster. Then he thinks he wakes up; he thinks he's safe. Then—*Frang!*—the monster leaps out at him, and it turns out he only dreamed he was waking up and he's still in the nightmare. Maybe it was like that, Tom thought: he had dreamed he was in heaven and then . . .

But he looked up and his eyes traveled around the room, his room. His familiar room with everything where it ought to be. And he knew this was real, this was really happening. It was no dream.

Okay, he thought. *Don't panic. Think. You're a reporter. Find the answer. Figure it out.*

He knew his mom's number by heart. She had told him once: *The problem with speed dials and contacts lists is that you never need to memorize a phone number.* And he had said: *Why would you ever want to memorize a phone number?* And she had said: *Well, in case you're lost somewhere without your phone.* And he had replied sarcastically: *Yeah, Mom. Like that's gonna happen!*

But all the same, Mom wasn't a big worrier, so when she did worry, it stuck in his head. He'd memorized her number one day, just in case.

He dialed the number now.

As the phone started ringing against his ear, he moved back out of the room, back down the hall to the stairs. He was just starting down the stairs again as the ringing stopped.

And there—hallelujah!—there was Mom, her voice coming over the phone: "Tom?"

Tom rolled his eyes with relief. "Mom! There you are!"

"Tom, can you hear me?" Mom said.

"Yeah, I'm right here," he said into the phone loudly. "Where are you?"

"Tom! Tom, are you hearing me?"

"Mom, I'm right here!" he shouted. "Can you hear me? I'm at home. Where are you?"

There was a pause. Then something awful happened, something that made Tom's stomach go hollow with fear. He was just coming off the last stair into the front hall again when he heard Mom say, "Oh, Tom, please say you hear me! Please! Please . . ."

Tom opened his mouth to answer her, but only a whisper came out. "Mom?"

Mom was crying. He could hear it. She was crying hard. And that was bad. Mom almost never cried. Mom was a girl, and a very girly girl, but there was something really tough about her, too, something really strong. She cried when they buried Burt. She cried when the lieutenant colonel handed her the folded flag from Burt's coffin, the overlong, coffin-sized flag that now hung on Tom's bedroom wall. She cried then, sure. Tom cried, too. Everybody cried, even the lieutenant colonel. But that's what it took—that's how much it took to make Mom break down in tears. Other than that, it just didn't happen.

Except that she was breaking down now on the phone.

"Tom, you have to hear me! You have to!" she said, her sobs almost overwhelming the words.

Tom practically shouted back at her, "I hear you, Mom! I'm right here! I'm right here! I can hear you! Where are you? What's the matter?"

"Oh, Tom, please!" Mom cried, almost hysterical now—and Mom never got hysterical, never. "Please answer me!"

Tom clutched at his own hair in frustration. "Mom, where are you? What's wrong? Tell me where you are! I hear you!"

And then there was a sound that made Tom's heart squeeze tight in his chest. That double beep.

He looked at the readout on the phone: *Connection lost.* "No!"

Tom shouted out loud in his frustration. Quickly, he pressed the Redial button. The phone sang out its series of tones and then began ringing again. It rang twice . . . three times . . .

"Come on!" Tom willed his mother to answer.

Where was she?

In the middle of the fourth ring, the ring broke off.

"Mom?" Tom said eagerly.

"You've reached Ann Harding's cell phone. Please leave a message after the tone."

Her voice mail!

The tone sounded. Tom started talking rapidly, urgently. "Mom, it's me. Listen. Where are you? I heard you before but you couldn't hear me. Everything's so bizarre here. Call me back as soon as you get this! Okay?"

He hung up. His unsteady hand slowly fell to his side.

What. Is. Going. On?

Has to be an explanation, he thought. *Has to be, has to be, has to be. There always is.*

But that horrible, horrible sound of his mother's frantic crying came back to him and he realized: even if there was an explanation, it wasn't going to be good.

Tom stood there, thinking, trying to figure out what to do next. His eyes moved slowly around the front hall. His gaze traveled over the large photo portrait that hung on the wall—right next to the hall closet so it was the first thing you saw when you came in. It was a photo of the three of them: Mom, Burt, and Tom. A blowup of the portrait they'd had taken for the church directory. Mom was sitting in a chair. Burt was behind her to the right, wearing his uniform. Tom was in a jacket and tie behind her to the left. Each of the brothers had one hand on Mom's shoulder. Tom's glance moved past the framed photo to the small wooden cross that hung beside it—then onto the sidelight beside the door, to the pane that held the gold star sticker that marked this as the home of a family that had lost someone in the war.

Tom gazed absently at the star for a minute—and then the focus of his gaze shifted and he looked through the glass to the outside.

The marine layer had thickened out there. The fog had crept in closer to the house. The whiteness hunkered and swirled over the edge of the grass. The end of the driveway was misted over, almost invisible.

Tom stared out, trying to think. He saw the fog shift a little.

Someone was standing there!

There was a woman standing in the street, standing in the mist, just at the very end of the driveway. The first human being he had seen all morning. She was a small woman, thirty or forty years old. Pale and thin. She was dressed in light colors—a white blouse, a tan skirt—so that she almost blended into the swirling white atmosphere. She didn't move. She didn't do anything. She just stood there, staring. Her face was expressionless—weirdly blank—almost completely empty of any feeling, as if she were sleepwalking or as if . . . as if she weren't alive at all.

Moment after moment, she didn't move. She just went on standing there, standing very still, her arms down by her sides. Standing and staring at the house. Staring straight at the sidelight. Staring straight at Tom.

Tom felt as if his heart had stopped beating. He gaped

out at the woman, his phone forgotten in his hand. The woman didn't move. The dead expression on her face didn't change. But now the fog began to blow and roll across her. The swirling white mist began to thicken around her. It began to cover her over. She began to fade into it, her features becoming dim, her figure becoming more shadowy, harder to see. As Tom watched, dumbstruck, she began to disappear from view.

No! thought Tom.

He grabbed the door, pulled it open, and rushed outside.

4.

Tom felt the cold and damp of the day on his face as he broke from the house. He moved quickly to the driveway, quickly down the driveway toward the street where the woman in the white blouse was standing. Even as he hurried toward her, she seemed to fade away from him, to fade back into the swirling fog.

"Hey, wait!" he shouted, waving his hand.

But the woman didn't answer him. With that same eerily dead look on her face, she slowly began to turn to one side.

"Hey!" Tom called, jogging faster down the driveway toward her. "Hey, hold on a second, would you?!"

No answer—and the woman started walking away.

Tom felt another sickening thrill of fear. Something was really wrong with this. Something about this woman was really wrong. The emptiness of her expression. The way she didn't answer him, didn't respond to his shouts at all. The slow, deliberate way in which she stepped now into the turning, moving mist.

Tom ran faster. As he neared the end of the drive, the fog began to close around him. He felt it, clammy on his face and his arms.

"Hold on!" he cried out to the woman again.

She seemed not to hear him. She took another step down the road, into the fog, away from him. Her figure grew dimmer as the whiteness closed over her. But then, suddenly, as Tom kept running toward her, she turned her head. She looked directly at him! The fog thinned for just a moment, and he got a good look at her face.

Tom gasped out loud. He had that feeling he got when an elevator went down too fast—as if he were falling but his stomach was staying in one place.

Because he knew her! He recognized her! He couldn't remember her name, but he remembered her voice, all right. He had just heard her voice a little while ago.

I need to talk to you. It's very important . . .

It was the woman who had called him just this morning. The woman whose call had woken him from his dream. He remembered her insistent voice over the phone . . .

Please!

. . . her voice reaching out to him through that strange static, reaching out urgently as if from someplace very far away.

But what was her name? He knew it. Why couldn't he remember?

"Wait, please!" he shouted.

But the woman only stared at him one instant more. Then she turned and walked into the fog and the fog gathered thickly around her. Tom had one last glimpse of her. Then she faded to a misty figure. Then the fog swallowed her, and she was gone.

Tom didn't hesitate. He ran after her. He plunged after her into the fog.

A moment—a step—and the murk of white surrounded him. The slimy damp chilled his skin. The thick mist cut off his vision almost entirely. For another second or two as he ran, he could see the curb beside the Colliers' lawn—then even that, barely a few yards away, disappeared under the churning marine layer.

All the same, at first, Tom didn't think about it. All he

thought about was catching up to the woman, finding out who she was, what she wanted. Over and above his fears, that pulse of curiosity—that need to get the answers—was pounding in him now. He was desperate just to talk to someone, just to ask some living person what on earth was going on.

He kept running. The woman had been moving so slowly, she couldn't have gotten far away. Even stumbling blindly through the mist as he was, Tom was sure to catch up to her if he stayed on the road.

But he didn't catch up to her. It was strange. More than strange. He ran for several more seconds, his sneakers slapping the macadam as he charged deeper and deeper into the ever-thickening mist. But there was no sign of her, no sign of anyone, no sign—he finally noticed—of anything at all.

He stopped, breathless. He stood, panting. He looked around him. Even in the cold damp of the fog, he felt himself begin to sweat.

He couldn't see anything now—nothing but the fog. He turned around in a full circle. The white mist was so thick it erased every detail from sight. He could make out a few inches of pavement around his feet and that was it. Still, he insisted to himself, still—how could that woman have gotten away from him? How could she have vanished like that, walking so slowly when he was running so fast?

"Hello?" he shouted—really loudly this time. "Hello? Where'd you go? Where are you?"

He listened, and finally—finally!—a noise answered him: a shuffling footstep.

He spun round to face the sound. There she was!

He could see her figure in the mist, not far away, just a shadow of a shadow really. But now, instead of fading from him, she seemed to be getting closer, the outline of her growing darker, more distinct.

"I'm over here . . . ," he began to shout to her, but even as the words passed his lips, his voice faded away to nothing.

Because now he realized: it wasn't her. That figure moving toward him. It wasn't the woman in the white blouse at all. It was someone else.

It was something else.

Tom narrowed his eyes and strained to see through the murk. The figure came toward him slowly, slowly growing clearer with every step. He could tell it wasn't the woman in the white blouse by the way it was moving. Instead of her slow but certain and steady pace, this figure had a sort of shambling limp. Its shoulders seemed hunched. Its arms hung and swung.

Tom almost called out again, but some instinct stopped him. He licked his lips. They were suddenly dry as dust.

He heard another sound and turned to his left. There

was another figure moving toward him from where the Staffords' hedges were supposed to be. Another shambling, limping shadow coming slowly toward him out of the fog.

And then another footstep to his right. And Tom turned and saw yet another shadow limping its way out of the mist from where the Colliers' lawn must've been.

Whatever they were, they were all around him.

Tom began to feel as clammy inside as the fog on his skin. The fear that swirled up out of the core of him was, in fact, like an inner fog. It filled his brain. It clouded his mind. He remembered that moment earlier in the day when he had come down the drive to get the newspaper, when he had looked into the swirling mist and had the bizarre thought that something was moving in there, that something was coming slowly toward him, shuffling slowly toward him. And now it was true. The figure he saw in front of him right now—the figures he saw to his left and right—they *were* shuffling toward him: slowly, relentlessly, and with that strange, hobbled, inhuman gait.

For another second, his reporter's curiosity pinned Tom to the spot.

What are they? What are they?

Then even his curiosity was overwhelmed by his terror—and he turned and ran.

5.

He ran without thinking. He couldn't have stopped himself if he tried. He was in pure panic mode now and just had to get back into the safety of his house. Back where he could think, back where he could clear his brain and return to some semblance of common sense and reality. Because this wasn't reality, this couldn't be reality, this was like . . .

Like a zombie apocalypse!

Yes! That's what it reminded him of exactly. Like one of those movies where the hero goes to sleep one night and wakes up to find that everyone on earth has died and come back as shambling, brain-eating, flesh-devouring monsters. And the fact that things like that didn't happen in real life was not reassuring—not reassuring at all—because he was just too frightened in that moment to care. He was too frightened even to think about anything but getting out of that fog and fast.

So he ran. Back through the clammy, roiling cloud. Back toward his house—back toward where he hoped his house was, anyway. He looked over his shoulder as he ran and saw the three shambling figures still behind him, still visible, but fading somewhat as he outpaced them, as they clumped after him slowly and he ran away as fast as he could.

He faced forward, plunging blindly through the shifting white. And now a noise of fear escaped him. Up ahead of him, he saw yet another figure—no, two more figures—two more men or whatever they were shambling toward him slowly from the other end of the street. They were moving slant-wise, moving to cut him off from his own driveway, he thought, to intercept him before he could reach his house.

Tom changed course, cutting to his left, hoping against hope that his driveway really was where he thought it was.

If he was right, he would beat the—the things—the creatures—whatever they were—he would beat them to the driveway and get to his house before they could get to him.

Through the cold, thickening, sickening clouds of panicked terror inside him, there suddenly came a laser-thin ray of hope. The fog was thinning. The edge of his driveway was dimly visible. He was heading in the right direction!

The shadows up ahead were still some distance away. The shadows behind him . . . He glanced back over his shoulder again. He could barely see them now. Yes! He was going to make it!

With new determination, he faced forward.

And one of the things was standing right beside him. It made an unholy sound and lunged at him out of the fog.

He hadn't seen it there until that instant. He hadn't noticed it creeping toward him from the right. Now, without warning, it was suddenly almost on top of him, mere yards away, its silhouette boldly clear behind the thinning curtain of mist. As Tom broke from the thickest depths of the fog into the clearer area at the bottom of his driveway, the thing let out that bizarre noise—a hollow, self-echoing shriek—and reached out to grab him.

Tom twisted his shoulder to avoid its grasp. A weirdly gnarled hand with long claws swept past him. For a single second, the creature's face emerged from the fog.

Tom only caught a glimpse of it, but that one glimpse made the terror in him blaze like an icy fire. The thing was not what he feared. It was not some human being who had turned into a zombie. It was not a human being at all.

The face Tom saw—or thought he saw—it flashed by him too quickly for him to be certain—was the face of a beast unlike any he had ever seen before. Its skin was ash-gray, darkened by patches of sickly red. Its semihuman features were strangely elongated, as if its head had been stretched top to bottom. Strands of greasy hair were strung across its mottled pate. Its nose was like a pit. Its cheeks were deeply sunken. Its mouth gaped open, the sharp teeth gleaming within. It would have almost seemed the face of a dead and rotting thing except that the eyes were sparkling with an eager, living cruelty.

It made that noise again. That horrible, somehow *hungry* noise. As its swiping claws missed Tom's shoulder, its hideous features came within inches of him. Tom cried out gruffly in disgust. Then the creature stumbled past him and staggered clumsily back into the depths of the fog, fading from sight.

The beast would surely turn around and try again, but Tom did not wait around to watch. He didn't slow down at all. He just kept running. A few more steps and he broke out of the mist. He felt the damp grip of the stuff release him as his front yard and his house came into view not far ahead. He raced wildly up the driveway, his sneakers slapping the pavement. He had a sense that the creatures were still after him, that they were shambling toward him from every side. But he didn't look, he didn't dare. He just kept running.

A few more strides to his front door. He was there, his hand on the knob. Now he was pulling the door open. Now he hurled himself inside. Now, at last, he slammed and locked the door behind him.

Panting, gasping, heaving in each rasping breath, he peered out the sidelight to see if the beasts were going to come after him. But no. There was nothing there now, nothing visible, anyway. He could see the driveway clear down to the end. The mist was as it was before, thick all around the edges of the lawn, but hanging back from his house itself as if the house and front lawn were in some kind of protective bubble.

Tom had a momentary, terrifying thought. What if—while he was out there—what if some of those things had gotten inside the house? What if one of them was creeping down the hall behind him, reaching out for his neck right now?

He spun around and stared at his own home wide-eyed. He listened, straining with every particle of himself to hear anything, anything moving, approaching.

And a voice came to him from down the hall: "Tom? Tom? Are you there?"

Tom's heart seized in his chest. The voice was coming from the kitchen.

"Tom?"

For a moment, he couldn't believe what he was hearing. He was too stunned to answer.

"Tom? Can you hear me?"

He knew that voice. Of course he did. He would know it anywhere.

"Tom?" she called to him again.

And with a wild rush of relief, Tom called back to her, "Marie!"

THE FIRST INTERLUDE

Was it only three weeks ago? It was. Tom had come out of his last class of the day—American History—and he knew at once that his life had changed forever. The latest issue of the *Sentinel* had come out. Lisa, the editor, had used her study period to put the dead-tree edition in the racks that stood at the hallway corners. Students were already standing around holding copies of the paper in their hands or reading the digital version on their tablets. Staring at the front page. Gaping at the story on the front page:

Sources: Tiger Champs Used Drugs. By Tom Harding

It was a shattering revelation. The Tiger team of three years ago—the team that had, against all odds and expectations, won the Open Division and claimed the state championship, the team that had made the school so proud—had cheated. Several of the linemen had illegally used anabolic steroids, the dangerous prescription drugs that made you bigger and stronger in the short term, even as they damaged your long-term health.

As Tom walked down the hall, the kids reading the paper looked up. They looked at him. Their faces darkened. They watched him pass with their eyes narrowed and their lips pressed together with rage. One guy—Mitchell Smith, a Tigers lineman—purposely slammed his shoulder into Tom's shoulder as he walked by, making Tom grunt in pain and reel back a step. No one protested the attack. No one said a word.

It was plain to see: they hated him. Everyone in the whole school hated him for writing that story.

When Tom reached the newspaper office, Lisa was already at the editor's desk. She was reading the angry comments about him that were piling up rapidly on the newspaper's website.

"Tom Harding should be kicked out of school for telling

lies about our heroes," one comment read. "He's just jealous because he's never done anything to make us proud. He's a moron and he's disgraced our school." Other comments weren't quite so kind.

Tom dropped heavily into the chair behind his desk. He felt hollow inside. He'd had a lot of bad days these last few months, and this was shaping up to be one of the worst of them.

The *Sentinel's* office was just a small room in the school's basement, down the hall from the gym. It was cramped in there. Hardly any space at all between his desk and Lisa's. The walls were papered with notices and notes and sched-ules and fragments of mock-up layouts pinned onto bulletin boards and taped onto the wall.

Lisa sat on her swivel chair, leaning forward to gaze into her monitor. She was a pug-nosed girl, with freckled cheeks and long, dark red hair. She wore glasses with black frames and small round lenses. Behind the lenses, her green eyes were smart and kind. She shook her head as yet another furious comment appeared on the site, and then another.

She glanced up at Tom with a look of sympathy. "They'll get over it, Tom," she said. "They can't stay angry forever." She did not sound very convincing, and Tom was not very convinced.

He tried to smile, but it didn't come off. He had expected

something like this—something—but not so much, so much rage against him, so much hatred. He knew that everyone in school loved the Tigers. But didn't they understand? He loved the Tigers, too! Even before he'd reached high school, he'd been their biggest fan. He didn't want to hurt them or soil their reputation. It was just . . . well, he was a reporter, and he had gotten hold of an important story. He had had no choice but to tell the truth, whether it went against his interests or not.

"People are like this, Tommy," said Lisa gently. "They blame the messenger for bringing the bad news."

He nodded. "I know."

"Will you be all right?"

He glanced at her. This time he managed to get one corner of his mouth to turn up. "Sure," he joked, "I never wanted to have any friends anyway."

Lisa smiled. "You have one, at least," she said.

Grateful, Tom was about to answer her when he sensed a new presence in the room and turned to the door. Instantly, he forgot whatever he'd been about to say to Lisa—he forgot Lisa entirely—and sat there silently, staring, openmouthed.

Marie—Marie Cameron—was standing in the doorway.

He had been in love with Marie since they were both in the third grade. She had been beautiful then, but she was wildly, glamorously beautiful now. Her blond hair poured down in ringlets framing her high cheeks, her button nose, and her Cupid's-bow mouth. Her blue eyes shone and sparkled. Her figure was slender and lush by heart-stopping turns. Her smile was dazzling, a kind of silent music.

Tom did not know how many times he had dreamed about going out with her, putting his arm around her, kissing her. But Marie had always been with Gordon Thomas—the head cheerleader and the football quarterback, so perfect for each other they were a walking cliché.

All the same, even though Tom knew he had no chance with her, his heart sank to think that Marie would hate him now for what he'd written about the team. The Tigers' drug use had taken place while Gordon was still in middle school—but it was Gordon's team now, and he'd be furious to see it publicly shamed. Since Marie was Gordon's girlfriend, Tom thought she would be furious, too.

She stepped toward him and Tom tensed, waiting for her to unleash her rage.

Instead, she lifted her hand—her small, white, perfect hand—and said, "Hey, Tom, I was hoping I'd find you here. Do you think you could give me a lift home?"

For a moment, he could only sit there, could only go on gaping at her silently like some kind of nutcase.

Then he leapt out of his chair so fast he nearly knocked it over.

———

He drove Marie home in the old yellow Mustang Burt had left behind when he went overseas. He wished he had cleaned out the ancient papers and fast-food bags lying all over the floor in the backseat, but whenever he was working on a story, he got so involved he forgot to do stuff like that. He must've apologized to Marie for the mess about a hundred times—and every time he turned to say the words to her, he was amazed to see her sitting there, real as life but far more beautiful, in his very own passenger seat.

They drove up into the hills, the Pacific Ocean falling away below them, the water gleaming under the afternoon sun.

Marie waved off his apologies. She said she didn't care about the messy car. Then she said: "I want you to know, I really admire what you did, Tom. Writing that story."

"Really? I thought you'd be ticked off like everyone else . . ."

"I'm not at all. I think it's brave to tell the truth like that. Not caring what anyone thinks of you. It's really brave."

Tom didn't answer. He didn't even glance at her—he didn't want her to see the look on his face. To have Marie tell him he was brave—it made up for all the nasty looks in the hall, all the nasty comments online, all of it.

"But what about Gordon?" he asked her. The words came out of his mouth as the thought came into his mind. "I mean, I know he didn't do anything wrong, but . . . it's his team. Isn't he angry at me, too?"

But Marie shrugged again. "I don't know how he feels. We haven't talked about it," she said.

The answer surprised him. It was almost as if she didn't care what Gordon thought. Tom didn't really want to question this, but it made him so curious he couldn't help himself. He had to ask: "Speaking of Gordon, how come he couldn't drive you home? Wasn't he around?"

"He's around," Marie said offhandedly. "But I wanted you to drive me, that's all. I feel like I don't get to see you enough."

This time Tom was so surprised he couldn't help but look over at her. She smiled. And what a sight that was. Amazing.

He stopped the Mustang in front of her house. It was a sprawling two-story mansion with white curving balconies overlooking the ocean. Really a massive palace of a place. Marie's father, Dr. Cameron, was one of the most important guys in town—and obviously one of the richest, too. He was always in the newspaper, serving on this board or that, or showing up at some big party for some big charity or other.

And there he was now, in fact, just stepping out of the black Mercedes parked in the driveway. He looked up and smiled at Tom and Marie and gave them a friendly wave. Marie waved back.

Then she turned to Tom. "I meant what I said," she told him. "I admire what you did. And I hope we can see each other more from now on."

Somehow Tom managed to hide the thrill he felt. He managed to sound almost cool and calm as he answered, "I would like that. I would like it a lot."

Marie gave him another smile—this one so brilliant it may have actually been illegal. "Good," she said. "Then we have a plan."

Tom watched her get out of the car. He watched her walk up the drive to join her father by the front door. He watched her turn and twinkle a final wave at him over her shoulder.

Amazing, he thought to himself. It was the only word he could come up with, and he thought it again and again: *Amazing*.

6.

arie!" he cried out now.

Wild-eyed, he hurried down the hall to her, the images of the shambling monsters out in the fog still filling his brain.

As he stepped into the kitchen, Marie leapt up from her chair at the round table in the breakfast nook. She rushed into his arms and he held her, his cheek against her golden hair.

"I'm so glad you're all right," she whispered into his chest.

Tom let his fear and panic melt into the warm press of her and the sweetness of her perfume. He closed his eyes for a moment, in relief and pleasure. When he opened them, he looked over Marie's head. Behind the table in the nook, the windows showed the backyard. Everything looked strangely normal out there. The mist was not as thick as it was out front. It obscured the sun, but Tom could still see the backyard grass and the hedges that bordered the Laughlins' property behind them. Most important, there were no semi-human shapes visible, no threatening figures shuffling and limping toward the house.

He held Marie away from him so he could look down into her face. "What about you?" he said. "Are you okay?"

She nodded, her crystal eyes glistening. "I've been so scared, though. So scared."

"Then you saw them? Those—those things in the fog. I'm not imagining them. You saw them, too."

Marie turned away from him. She put her hand to her face, rubbed her eyes wearily. "I don't know what I saw. I was so terrified. I just ran. I just ran to get here, to find you."

Even in his fear and confusion, the words filled Tom's heart. Now, at least, he had a job to do: protect Marie. Keep her safe. Even if nothing else made sense, there was a mission that could guide his actions.

"I think we should get in my car," he said. "Get out of here. They could attack the house any minute."

Marie turned back to him and shook her head. "I don't think so. I don't think they can leave the fog. I think we're safe in here for now. Safer than we'd be outside, anyway."

Tom thought about it. "Do you know what's happening?" he asked her. "Is it happening all over? I haven't seen anyone else. No one human, anyway."

Marie turned back to him and shook her head. The tears still shone in her eyes. "I'm not sure . . ."

"I called my mom. I reached her, but she couldn't hear me."

"I know. I talked to my father," said Marie. "We didn't have a good connection, but I could make out some of what he was saying. He was the one who sent me here. He said you were the only person who could help us."

"Me? I don't even know what's going on. Those monsters out there—it's like—it's like we're in a zombie apocalypse."

Marie gave a weak laugh. "I don't think that's what it is."

Tom himself managed a small laugh at the idea. "Right. Probably not."

He suddenly felt exhausted. He moved to one of the chairs by the round table and sank down into it. He stared out the window without really seeing anything. He was thinking about that thing—that thing with the hideous face—its claws snatching at him from the fog, nearly grabbing him before he even saw it.

What was it?

He shook his head. "You know what it is like, though?" he said softly, almost as if he were speaking to himself, working it out in his mind. "It's like one of those movies or TV shows where strange things keep happening and after a while, you start to realize that none of it is real. You know? It's too weird. It can't be real. It has to be a dream or something. Or maybe the lead character is really dead or he's gone crazy or somebody slipped him some kind of drug and he's having a hallucination. You know what I mean? You think that's what this is: a dream or a hallucination? Or do you think we're actually dead?"

He glanced over at her. He took comfort from the warmth and sympathy in her gaze. She stepped forward and put her hand gently on his shoulder. "I'm pretty sure we're not dead," she said. "Not yet, anyway."

He nodded slowly. "But then what?" he said. "What's happening, Marie? There has to be a reasonable explanation. Doesn't there?"

Marie now sat down in the chair in front of him. She took his two hands in her hands. He found her cool touch soothing. They sat facing each other. He looked deep into her eyes. Even now—still haunted by the memory of those creatures

ranging through the fog—by that clawed hand reaching for
him—by that deformed and hideous face looming in front
of him—even now, the sight of Marie, the sweet beauty of
her, made his heart swell. He could not remember a time
when he hadn't longed to be with her.

"Do you remember the monastery in the woods?" she
asked him.

The question was so unexpected, so odd, that it was
a moment before he could take it in, a moment before he
could answer. "Sure," he said uncertainly. "The Catholic
one. The retreat. The one that burned down. St. Mary or
something . . ."

"Santa Maria," said Marie.

"Yeah, that's it."

The Santa Maria Monastery Retreat had been a com-
pound of Spanish-style buildings set around a pretty chapel
deep in the forest up on Cold Water Mountain. It was gone
now. The so-called Independence Fire that had scorched the
hills last July—that had consumed acres and acres of woods
up there and destroyed more than a hundred houses—had
reduced Santa Maria's stately buildings, valuable antiques,
and tranquil gardens to charred ruins.

"What about it?" said Tom. "What's the monastery got
to do with anything?"

"My father says you have to go up there. He says that's

where the answers are and where you're supposed to be right now. He says if you can get to Santa Maria, you can bring all this craziness to an end."

Tom stared at her. "But why?" he said. It made no sense. Tom would do just about anything to get answers, to find out the truth about all this, but . . . go back outside? Out into the fog where those—those things were? And up into the woods on Cold Water Mountain? To the ruins of the monastery? "How can that possibly help?"

Holding his hands firmly in hers, Marie shook her head. "I'm not sure. Like I said, our connection wasn't that good. But Daddy said it was important. Urgent, even. He said once you get to the monastery, you'll know what you have to do to bring this to an end."

As Tom went on staring at her, thoughts raced through his mind. *Why the monastery? Why the mountain?* He was trying to make sense of it. Was it possible that what was happening here was some sort of supernatural, spiritual event? Were those creatures in the fog some kind of demons? Did he have to get up to Santa Maria to call on the power of God to fight them or to call on the angels or something? But why the monastery? And why him? His family had always gone to Hope Church around the corner. It was nondenominational. They weren't even Catholic!

"I don't get it," he was about to say—but before he could,

his phone rang in his pocket. The guitar riff: "The Fightin' Side of Me."

Tom tried to reach for the phone, but Marie gripped his hands even tighter. He saw her eyes flash to his pocket, to the place where the phone was singing.

"Don't answer that!" she said, her voice a frightened whisper.

Confused, he worked one hand free. "What do you mean? I have to answer it. It might be my mom."

He reached into his pocket. He felt the phone vibrating there.

Marie looked at him urgently. "It's not," she said. "It's not your mom. I know it! Don't answer, Tom. I mean it. Just do what Daddy said. Just get to the woods, get to the monastery. That's where the answers are! That's what you want, isn't it? Answers. That's what you're always . . ."

Tom pulled the phone out. He checked the readout: *Number blocked.*

"I'm serious," said Marie. "Don't."

The urgency of her tone made him hesitate a second. But finally he said, "I have to. It really might be my mom."

Marie let go of his other hand. She dropped back against the chair and let out a long breath, giving up.

Tom answered the phone. "Hello?"

There was a silent pause. And then—Tom's heart sped

up as he heard the static—that same odd, distant static he'd heard first thing this morning when the phone woke him. Again, it sounded like it was coming from somewhere far away, some alien place, some frightening place he could not imagine. And again, as he listened, he heard that voice, that woman's voice, trying to reach him through the noise.

"I need to talk to you. It's so important. I need . . ."

Tom leaned forward, gripping the phone hard in his sweating fingers. He knew that voice—he knew it! It was that woman. The woman in the white blouse who had been standing down at the base of the driveway. The woman who had gazed at him with that peculiarly blank, dead expression—and then vanished into the fog. He didn't know how he knew it was her, but he knew. Why couldn't he remember her name?

"What do you want?" Tom said to her, nearly shouting over the static. "I can barely hear you. What do you want?"

"I need to talk to you . . . ," the woman said again, but already the static was closing over her voice as the fog had closed over her figure.

"What do you want?" Tom shouted, more desperately this time as he heard her fading. "Why didn't you wait for me in the driveway? Why didn't—"

But the phone beeped twice: *Connection lost.* She was gone.

Tom cried out in frustration.

"Tom . . . ," Marie began to say. "Tom, listen to me. You have to listen—"

But before she could finish, another voice interrupted her.

"This is your mission! This is what I've been trying to tell you about all along . . . The Warrior . . . Do you remember the Warrior?"

Burt! It was his brother's voice! It was coming from the basement again. What was happening here? What was going on?

Tom leapt up out of his chair. Marie jumped up, too, jumped up so quickly her chair fell over behind her, banging loudly against the floor.

"Tom," she whispered. "Don't . . ."

"That's Burt," he said. "Don't you hear it? That's Burt's voice."

"It's not. It can't be. You know that. Burt is dead," said Marie.

"I heard him before. The same way. From down in the basement."

"Tom, listen to me, do not go down there."

Tom stood looking at her, uncertain. He licked his dry lips. He wanted to help her, to keep her safe. He wanted to do what she said. But it was Burt . . .

"Marie, I don't understand any of this," he said. "Do you

know more than you're telling me? Is there something you don't want me to know?"

"All I know is that you have to go to the monastery," she answered urgently. "*That's* where the answers are. You have to find them. You can't wait any longer. You have to go there now."

But Tom could hear Burt shouting again: "This is what I tried to teach you. This is what you have to do . . ."

And then he said, "This is your mission, Tom."

Tom started. Did Burt just call him by name? From the TV? How was that possible? He had to know—he had to find out—where the voice was coming from.

He looked helplessly at Marie. "I've got to look," he said.

He turned away from her. He went to the basement door.

Marie called out behind him in a sharp tone of voice he'd never heard her use before. "Tom! Listen to me! Please! You don't always have to know everything! You've got to stop this!"

He looked at her. He saw the fear and frustration flashing in her eyes, her bowed mouth twisting in a strange and ugly way. But it didn't matter. He heard Burt downstairs.

"Remember the Warrior, Tom."

He had to go. He pulled open the door.

Marie shouted at him: "Tom, I mean it! Don't!"

Tom flipped the light switch. He left Marie in the kitchen and thundered quickly down the stairs.

He hit the basement floor and spun around the corner into the family room, moving fast. He saw the side of the television. He heard Burt's voice coming from the speakers: "This is what you have to understand! This is what I have to get you to understand . . ."

His brother sounded so present, so real—so alive!—that it made Tom hurt inside to hear him. He missed his brother so much it was like a physical pain.

He needed to get around to the front of the TV. He needed to see Burt's face, to see what he was doing on the video before the whole thing vanished again as it had earlier, before the voice went silent and Burt was gone.

He took a quick step forward.

"All along," said Burt, "this was what I was trying . . ."

And then, sure enough, the voice stopped, mid-sentence. And the next moment there was another voice: "Dr. Cooper to the ER—stat!"

"No!" shouted Tom.

He hadn't been fast enough. There was that stupid doctor show again!

And yes, there it was. As he got in front of the TV, he saw the same scene that had been on before.

The nurse was shouting, "Single GSW to the chest! Clear Trauma One."

The doctors and nurses and aides were crowding around

the gurney, rolling the gurney frantically down the hospital hallway to the emergency operating room. The patient—the person lying wounded on the gurney—was obscured by the crush of bodies around him as they all hurtled together down the corridor shouting urgently to one another.

"How's the pulse?"

"Sixty and falling fast!"

Exasperated, Tom's eyes went heavenward and his shoulders slumped in defeat. The monsters in the fog. The images on TV. Marie telling him to leave everything behind and go to the monastery. What was happening? What was it all about?

He looked at the TV again. The scene had changed now. The doctors and nurses and aides had pushed the gurney around the corner into a trauma alcove. They were leaning over the patient on the gurney, preparing to lift him onto the operating table.

"On three," said a doctor. "One, two, three!"

All together, as Tom watched, they hoisted the bloody form off the gurney and laid him on the table. When they were done, the cluster of people broke apart, each hurrying into a different corner of the little space, each turning to his own chore, wrangling his own piece of equipment. One nurse grabbed a tray of surgical instruments. A surgeon pulled on a sterile gown. Another nurse hooked up an oxygen tank. For a moment, as they worked, the patient lay alone on the table with no one around him, no one blocking him from view, so that Tom could finally see him, see his face.

The sight was as shocking as anything he had seen this whole shocking day. Tom's mouth fell open and the breath came out of him as quickly as if he had been punched. He stared unblinking at the TV, unable to believe what he was looking at, unable for a second or two even to comprehend it.

The patient on the gurney: It was Tom. It was Tom himself.

7.

The sight of himself on the TV screen, the sight of himself as a character in his mom's favorite medical show, hit Tom so hard he actually took a step back. He went on staring, went on gaping, second after second as the scene unfolded. He watched as the patient—himself—lay on the table unconscious, his eyes closed. He saw with a growing nausea that his shirt was covered in blood, the stain spreading all the way from his collar to his belt buckle.

And now the nurses were cutting his clothes away with a knife. The place where the bullet had ripped into his body was exposed, his flesh gory and torn. A nurse was stuffing a tube into his throat—it made Tom gag just to watch it. Another nurse was jamming a needle into his arm—he practically felt the sting.

Then, most horrifying of all, a doctor, his face obscured behind a surgical mask, stepped forward and set a scalpel against his skin—Tom's skin. They were going to cut him open on television right before his own eyes. Tom—standing there in the family room, staring at the TV—could almost feel the cold touch of the blade against him.

But all at once the scene went blank. The television turned itself off.

The sudden darkness on the screen snapped Tom's trance. He shook himself as if he were waking up. Without thinking, he turned and found the remote on one of the chairs, lifted it, pointed it at the TV, and tried to turn the show on again. The prospect of watching himself cut open made him sick to his stomach, but he had to know what happened next, had to find out what all this meant.

Training his intense blue eyes on the TV screen by sheer force of will, he pressed the Power button. Nothing happened. Pressed it again—nothing. He tossed the remote back down onto the chair.

Think, he told himself. *Figure it out. Finding answers is what you do. Find them!*

But how could he? His own image on the TV. Burt calling him by name. Marie urging him to the burned-out retreat in the woods. Monsters in the fog. How could he put any of it together? How could he make sense out of any of it?

Marie, he thought. She—or her father—was the only one who seemed to know anything. He had to get back to her, find out more. Why did he have to go to the monastery? She must know. She must know *something* she wasn't telling him.

He raced back to the stairs, back up the stairs. He reached the top and pushed through the door into the kitchen. He stopped short on the threshold, staring.

Marie was gone.

The breakfast nook was empty. The kitchen was empty. Other than that, everything seemed to be exactly as he had left it. The chairs were in disarray. The one chair Marie had knocked over was still lying on the floor. Tom could even still smell a trace of Marie's perfume lingering in the air. It was as if she'd only just now left the room.

"Marie?" he called out. "Marie!"

But there was no answer, and once again the house had that feeling of complete emptiness.

He stepped to the hallway and called again.

"Marie!"

But the hall was empty. He knew she was gone.

Tom felt the bizarre events of the day spinning through his mind, ideas spinning through his mind as if they were trying to put themselves into the right order, looking for the pattern in which they fit together.

It's not a dream, Marie had told him. *It's not a hallucination. You're not dead. You're not mad. Go to the monastery. That's where the answers are.*

What did she know? What was it she wasn't saying?

His thoughts whirling, he turned back to the kitchen. And as he turned, his thoughts stopped.

Something was off. Different. His eyes went over the empty room. He had been wrong before. He had thought the kitchen was just the way he'd left it. But it wasn't. Not exactly. Something had changed. But what? What was it?

He couldn't tell. He stood still, looking the place over. There was the table, as before. The chairs in their skewed positions, the one fallen over. The sink, the cupboards, the door across the way that led into the dining room, the stove on the opposite wall—everything familiar, everything unchanged, a scene so normal that it made Tom ache for all the ordinary mornings when he would wake up and come downstairs to find his mom in here, making breakfast.

But something was definitely different. What was it?

His searching glance went from corner to corner. The cabinets, the basement door . . . back around to the table again, sitting empty there in the breakfast nook with the window behind it . . .

He stopped. That was it. The window.

The fog.

When he had come in here before, when he had first found Marie sitting at the table, he remembered he could see the backyard outside. There was mist out there, but it was thin. The scene was much clearer than it was out on the street, where the marine layer was so thick you could barely see a few feet in front of you.

Now, though, that had all changed. The fog had come in dense and close. It was pressed hard against the window-panes. The glass was white, completely misted over, dripping with moisture. The backyard was now totally invisible.

Tom moved toward the window slowly. Fear and curiosity were warring within him—and the fear was winning. Up until now, he'd had the feeling that the house was somehow protected, somehow surrounded by a sort of safety zone that kept the fog—and the monsters in the fog—at bay.

But he saw now it wasn't so. The fog was right up against the house, a wall of white, impenetrable.

Did that mean the monsters were also close?

Frightened as he was, he had to find out—had to. He

moved toward the breakfast nook. He edged around the table. He leaned in to the window, pressed his forehead against the cool glass, trying to peer out.

He could see nothing. Stillness. Fog, thick and swirling. Or wait . . . Was something there? Did something just move? Tom squinted, peering harder. Tendrils of fog turned and curled and the whiteness seemed to thin a little. The view began to clear.

A creature was staring back at him through the window, its sharp teeth bared, its cruel eyes gleaming.

Tom had only a second to react—only a second to step backward.

Then the window exploded as the creature lunged at him through the shattering glass.

8.

The creature burst through the window with an echoing screech that obliterated thought. It was a screech of ungodly hunger. It twisted the monster's already hideous features into a fanged, snarling portrait of pure brutality.

Tom stumbled backward in terror, his arms pinwheeling. His side banged painfully into the edge of the breakfast table. The jolt knocked him off-balance and he went down on one knee, grabbing hold of one of the chairs to break his fall. The creature—half inside the house and half out—strained and reached for him and screamed again, trying to clamber the rest of the way through the window to get at him. Tom saw the wicked, razor-sharp claws on its fingers stretched out toward him, inches away from his face.

Holding on to the chair, Tom quickly dragged himself to his feet. For a second, the monster withdrew its reaching hands and grabbed hold of the windowsill in order to propel itself inside. Completely ignoring the shards of glass that lanced into the flesh of its palms and arms, the beast started to climb in.

Tom lifted the chair with both hands. He brought it back over his shoulder. Swung it as hard as he could at the monster's face.

One of the chair legs connected with the beast's head. The thing gave an ugly grunt and tumbled backward out of the house, vanishing into the fog again.

But the fog was pouring into the kitchen like smoke. Tom knew it would be only moments before the monster tried to come in again.

And now he heard the sound of shattering glass in the living room.

"Oh no," he whispered.

They were breaking in everywhere.

He dropped the chair. He rushed across the kitchen to the far door. He looked through—through the dining room—into the living room at the front of the house.

He thought he had been afraid before. He thought he had been afraid out in the fog when the creature had attacked him. That was nothing compared to this. Now the fear was like a raging fire inside him. It nearly burned his will away. It nearly left him weak and helpless.

Three of the things were crawling, clawing, climbing into the house. They had smashed the living room windows— the windows that ran all across the front wall—they had smashed all of them, and the fog was pouring through the openings. Second by second, the room was filling with white, swirling mist and the three creatures were coming in with it. They were scrabbling over the jagged shards of glass and tumbling through. One landed on the sofa, two fell to the floor. They all climbed slowly and clumsily to their feet. They looked around them with gleaming eyes.

They were searching—searching for Tom.

Tom ran right toward them. It cost him every ounce of courage he had, but he ran right through the dining room, right past the dining room table and into the living room, right at the beasts. It was the fastest way to get back to the front stairs—and the stairs were the only hope of survival he had. The kitchen was filling with fog behind him. The living room was growing misty in front of him. If he stayed where he was, the creatures would come crashing in through every window till the house was full of them and he would have nowhere to make a stand. Upstairs, at least he had a chance.

The hunched, grunting creatures spotted him at once as he raced toward them. They came to attention like hunting dogs when they get the scent of game. For a second, they went rigid, their horribly distorted faces twisting, their sunken nostrils flaring. Then they let out a hollow shriek of triumph—and they charged.

They moved slowly with their slumped, lumbering, limping gaits. Tom was already racing past them and heading for the front hall as they made their move. The monster closest to him reached out, and Tom felt the tip of one of its claws brush his arm. He dodged out of its way. The terror of the near miss gave him fresh agility and speed. He was past the thing before it could try again to grab him.

There was the front door now, the front hall, the stairs. He'd almost made it. He rushed through the connecting doorway, out of the living room, into the foyer. He began to reach for the newel-post to pull himself up the steps.

But as he did, the sidelight next to the front door burst. A clawed hand shot in and grabbed hold of him.

Tom saw the furred fingers close around his wrist. He felt the long claws slashing his flesh. He saw the pocked, elongated, skull-like face of the thing pressing through the hole in the sidelight. He saw the monster's eyes gleaming with cruelty and anticipation as it gripped him and began to pull him toward itself. Tom thought his heart would stop with sheer horror.

He tried to yank himself free, but the beast was strong—and worse than that: the creature's touch was somehow poisonous. The minute its hand wrapped around him, the minute its claws slashed him, Tom felt a swirling darkness enter his mind. He felt himself losing strength.

The beast held him fast, trying to pull him toward the sidelight. The fog poured in around him and his mind grew foggy, too. With every second, Tom felt himself becoming weaker. Out of the corner of his eye, he saw the monsters in the living room humping toward him. He heard them grunting and gasping. He saw their eyes gleaming, their teeth bared.

The monster at the sidelight continued to hold him and the fog swirled around him and the dark poison swirled through his brain. Tom wasn't even sure he wanted to fight anymore. So what if they got him? What was the worst thing that could happen, anyway? At least if they killed him, it would put an end to this day of horror and confusion . . .

His will was seeping away.

The beast leaning in through the window gibbered

wildly and kept trying to pull the weakening Tom toward him. Tom's legs went wobbly. His eyes rolled in his head as he began to lose consciousness. He saw the portrait on the wall, tilting and spinning. His mom. His brother. He saw the cross hanging beside it.

"Fight them! Fight them off! Despair is never an option!"

Tom shook his head, trying to clear it. Was that Burt?

"Don't give them even half a chance. Remember the Warrior . . ."

It was! It was Burt! On the television set again. His voice dim, far away but still shouting up to him from the basement.

"Don't give in! That's just the poison talking! Come on! You're my brother! You do not surrender! The Warrior, Tom!"

A surge of strength went through him. Tom gave a roar and pulled himself free of the monster's grasp, ignoring the claws that sliced his arm.

At once the poison seemed to leave his body, the darkness seemed to drain out of his mind. Light and alertness flooded through him and he was fully awake again.

With the new energy surging through his muscles, he started moving. Just as the monsters clumped out of the living room into the front hall, just as they began to close in on him, he shot up the stairs as fast as he could go.

He took the stairs two and three at a time. He broke free of the fog. It fell away behind him. The shuffling, limping monsters clustered on the stairs beneath him, bumping into the walls, bumping into one another, unable to rise above the level of the mist.

Tom was at the second-floor landing—was racing down the hall toward his room. Another moment and he was through his bedroom door. He slammed it shut. Locked it. Seized hold of the dresser with both hands. Dragged it across the floor and shoved it against the door, barricading himself inside.

He was safe—for now.

9.

anting hard, Tom leaned against the dresser. His fore-arm stung from where the creature's claws had dug into him. There was blood soaking into his sweatshirt sleeve. The fear inside him was so powerful it was sickening. For a moment, he thought he was actually going to throw up. But he remembered his brother's voice shouting to him from the basement.

Fight them! Fight them off! Despair is never an option!

Shouting to him, calling him by name, as if it weren't just Burt on a video but the real Burt, really there, still alive.

Remember the Warrior, Tom!

Tom didn't know how it was possible for his brother to reach out to him from the grave like that. But right this minute, with everything so crazy, he didn't care. Nothing made sense now, so he might as well cling to the sound of that familiar voice he missed so much. He fought off the fear and the sickness. He gritted his teeth, and his mouth twisted as a low growl of determination came out of him.

He had to do something. Now. The beasts were still out there. The fog was rising. They would rise with it, come up the stairs, down the hall. They'd be at the door soon, any second. He had to find a way out of here. Find a way to get help.

Tom looked around at his bedroom for something he could use: the computer on the desk, the window by the bed, the sports pennants on the wall, the framed newspaper pages . . .

"Sources: Tiger Champs Used Drugs."

Something flashed through his mind. Some fragment of memory. Why couldn't he grasp it? He had to think . . .

Go to the monastery, Tom. That's where the answers are.

For a moment, Tom felt as if everything were on the verge of making sense . . .

Then the creatures reached his bedroom, and all his thoughts were scattered.

The first *thud* was soft, as if one of the beasts had stumbled coming down the hallway and fallen against the door. The noise was so faint Tom might have pretended to himself he hadn't really heard it.

But then the thing started mewling. That high-pitched, weirdly echoing sound was unmistakable. Tom took an involuntary step back as a fresh wave of fear went over him. He stared at the door.

The doorknob began to turn.

Tom heard the clicking of long claws against the metal. The knob turned tentatively at first. Once this way, once that. Then again. Then it clicked back and forth harder— back and forth. Then the knob began to rattle as the creature grew frustrated. The door began to shiver on its hinges . . .

Tom gasped as the door leapt in its frame. One of the things started pounding on the wood, slamming the wood— it sounded like with its open hand—again and again. Then it stopped. But the next noise went up Tom's spine and made his teeth ache. Scratching. Long claws were digging into the surface of the door, trying to rip their way through. Then there was more pounding—steady pounding now. Tom heard grunts, gasps, small animal shrieks out in the hall. How many of them were out there? He couldn't tell.

The snarling got louder. The pounding on the door got more insistent. The dresser that barricaded the door began to shiver.

Eyes wide, Tom turned this way and that, looking for some way out. The window . . .

He crossed the room to the window. Peered outside.

His bedroom looked out on the backyard. He could see the fog lying over the small square of grass. At first he couldn't make out much more than the ruffled whiteness. It was like staring down into clouds from an airplane.

But then he saw them.

There must have been nearly a dozen of them out there, dim hulking shadows ranging back and forth through the mist. Some were climbing into the house through the broken windows. Others were moving in slow, stumbling circles right below him, as if they were waiting for him to try to climb out and escape.

The pounding on the door continued behind him. And the growls and snorts and shrieks out in the hall continued, too. Grimly, Tom looked over his shoulder and saw the door rattling and the dresser trembling. The barricade couldn't hold forever. The creatures were going to come bursting in, and soon.

Tom prayed for help as he scrabbled in his pocket for his cell phone. *Please, God, help me, help me . . .*

He fished his phone out. His hands trembling, he quickly called up the number pad and keyed in 911. He raised the phone to his ear. Waited. But there was nothing. There was no sound. Quickly, he lowered the phone. Looked desperately at the readout. He felt his stomach go sour again as one of the creatures out in the hall gave a loud echoing cry and hit the bedroom door full force.

No bars on the phone. No reception.

He quickly stuffed the phone back in his pocket. He went to the computer on the desk. His fingers were so unsteady, he had to try three times before he could call up his browser. Maybe he could raise a friend, or contact the police by FaceTime or Skype or even e-mail. Something. Anything. He had to reach anyone he could.

He waited for the browser page to load. What was taking so long? A monster in the hallway let out another soul-withering shriek and crashed into the door so hard Tom thought the wood would splinter and the door would fly off its hinges.

"Come on! Please!" he whispered at the computer.

But the only answer was the words that now appeared on the laptop's screen: *Connection timed out*. He didn't even bother to try again. He knew the Internet was down.

He was trapped—trapped in here. Trapped in his room. With the creatures gathered out in the hall, trying to break in. With more of them on the ground outside, circling beneath his window in the mist.

There was no escape.

The monsters in the hallway roared and pounded on the door. What could he do? What could he do?

Remember the Warrior . . .

The Warrior!

All at once, Tom did remember—and the memory was like a little flame inside him. The Warrior. Of course.

He stepped to his closet. He reached into the dark at the back. He touched the cool metal of his aluminum baseball bat. He didn't play much anymore, but he'd never let his mom give the bat away. He brought it out. Read the label. *A Louisville Slugger Warrior.* Burt had given it to him for his birthday one year—Tom couldn't remember which year, which birthday it was. It was a good one, though. Burt had taken him out to the park the next day. He had pitched to him and given him tips on how to swing, how to play the game.

Was this what Burt was trying to get him to remember?

Well, he had it now. It wasn't much of a weapon, but somehow just the feel of it in his hand gave him courage. The creatures might break down the door, but the doorway was narrow. They could only come through one at a time, two at most. Maybe he could use the bat to fight them off, keep them at bay—for a while, anyway—who knew how long he could hold them? Even if they broke through eventually—even if they killed him—he'd at least have the satisfaction of de-braining some of them on his way out. A little payback for all this terror.

He returned with the bat to the bedroom door, posted himself in front of the dresser barricade. He gripped the handle of the bat in one hand—the bloody hand the monster had grabbed. He cradled the barrel in the other. He tried to ready himself.

The door continued to jump in its frame. The beasts continued to make those awful noises out in the hall. Tom's heart beat so hard, so loudly, the pulse of it filled his head. He waited. He waited for the door to give way, waited for the beasts to start coming through, waited, as the seconds ticked off one by one, for the final battle to begin.

Then, with shocking suddenness, the noises stopped. All of them. The pounding. The snarling and growling and shrieking in the hall. The rattle of the shivering dresser. All the noises stopped altogether. Only the thudding of Tom's heart continued, filling his mind as he went on staring at the door, as he went on gripping the bat in his sweating hands.

Come on, he thought. *I'm ready for you!*

But there was only silence. Silence and suspense—suspense worse than the terror.

Then—so surprising—so frightening it went through Tom's body like an electric shock—a man spoke from behind him, from right inside the room.

"Tom," he said quietly.

10.

Tom spun around so fast he nearly lost his balance. The voice seemed to have been coming from his desk. But there was no one there.

Yet as Tom stared at the empty desk chair, the man spoke again: "Listen to me, Tom."

The voice was coming from the computer. The monitor had gone dark now. But Tom saw something flicker in that darkness. A faint, failing light. A suggestion of static. And a figure—yes—a silhouette, barely visible.

"Everything will be all right," the figure said. "If you just do what I tell you to do."

The man had a deep voice—deep and mellow. Even in that shocking moment, it had a warm, calm tone that Tom found somehow reassuring.

"The creatures are gone now," said the figure quietly. "You're safe—for the moment, anyway."

"Who are you?" Tom said—he could barely muster a whisper.

"I'm your friend," said the dim silhouette. It could hear him! It could answer him. "I'm here to help you through this situation."

Tom took one quick glance at the door. It was still quiet out there. No more pounding. No more scratching or screaming. He turned back to face the computer. He dared to take a step toward it.

"What do you mean?" he said. "How can you help me? What can you do?"

The monitor flickered. For a moment, the man's silhouette was almost distinct. Tom thought he saw the faint glow of the man's eyes, watching him. The eyes made him feel cold. Goose bumps rose on his arms.

"You already see what I can do," the man responded quietly. "The hall is empty, isn't it? Go out there. Look out the window. The malevolents are gone."

"Malevolents?"

"Yes, it means—"

"I know what *malevolent* means," said Tom. "Evil."

"Evil. Yes," said the man calmly. "And they're gone, aren't they?"

Tom returned to the window, looked out. The fog was still thick out there, but the things he had seen moving in the depths of the whiteness were no longer visible. He nodded uncertainly, moving back to his post at the door. "Yeah. I guess. They seem to be gone. I don't see them at least, or hear them."

"They're gone. Believe me. I've sent them away."

"You did," said Tom. "You can do that? You can control them?"

"I can. For a time."

A rumble of thunder sounded outside. Tom glanced at the window just as a heavy rain started to fall. The drops pattered hard against the pane, streaking the glass as they rolled down. Tom faced the computer on the desk. There was a flash of lightning. The flash brightened the whole room for a shuddering second—and weirdly, it seemed to light up the depths of the computer screen as well. For that one instant, Tom seemed to see the man on the screen more clearly: a lean, dark, handsome face; high cheekbones; a thin smile; bright eyes, full of sharp intelligence. There was nothing particularly wrong-looking about him. Yet another chill went through Tom at the sight of him. The feeling was quickly gone and Tom pretended to himself he'd never felt it. The thing was: he needed help—badly—and the man in the computer was the only help on hand. He couldn't afford to distrust him.

"Who are you?" Tom said.

"I told you: I'm your friend. My name doesn't matter."

"Well, how can you control those things? The malevolents? How did you make them go away?"

"It doesn't matter how."

"It matters to me. It doesn't make sense."

"Yes, you hate that, don't you? When things don't make sense. You always want to figure them out. But you know, just because you don't understand something doesn't mean it can't be understood."

Tom had to acknowledge the truth of that. He didn't really understand calculus either, but he assumed it made sense to somebody.

"Do you know why they're here? These malevolents," he asked now. "Do you know how they got here?"

"I know," said the man quietly.

"Well, tell me!" Tom nearly cried out. "What's going on? Please!"

The man gave a low hum of sympathy. He said, "Yes. You want answers. That's your nature. You don't like lies.

You don't like secrets. You never met a mystery you didn't want to solve."

"So help me, then," said Tom.

"I'm trying, Tom. But some mysteries are very deep. Why is there evil at all, for instance? Why did Burt have to die? What's happening to you now? If you want the solutions to puzzles like those, you have to go the extra mile."

Tom shook his head, trying to work through his confusion. "What's it got to do with Burt? And what extra mile? What do you mean? What do I have to do to find out what's happening?"

"You have to do what Marie told you to do," said the man in his gentle, almost hypnotizing tone. "You have to go to the monastery. The answers are there."

"The monastery . . ." Tom gripped the baseball bat harder in his frustration. "Look, if you know so much, how about you just tell me the answers?"

"Because that's not the way it works," said the man gently. "You have to find the answers yourself. You have to face them yourself. The truth is not always easy, Tom. Sometimes it's even horrific. It's not enough to be told. You have to grasp it with your whole mind. You have to accept it with your whole heart. No one can do that for you."

Tom gave another hesitant nod. He had to acknowledge this, too. "Yeah. Yeah, I guess that's true."

"It is true. You know it is."

Lightning flickered at the window again and Tom turned to watch it. He kept watching until the lightning was gone and the low growl of thunder followed. He didn't admit it to himself, but the truth was he didn't want to see the computer screen light up again. He didn't want to see the man's face again so clearly. Something about the dude creeped him out.

The lightning faded. Tom looked at the computer. It was dark. Silent.

"What do you want me to do?" he asked.

The man's voice answered from the speaker, reassuringly calm and mellow. "Go to the monastery. The path is clear for now, but you have to hurry. I can't keep the beasts away forever."

Tom tried one more time to get something out of this guy. "At least tell me what I'm looking for. Tell me where my mom is. Is she all right?"

"The monastery, Tom," said the man quietly. "All the answers are at the monastery."

Tom cast a wary glance at the door. "And if I go out, I'll be safe? The monsters are gone? I can get where I'm going?"

"The monsters are gone. Everything will be fine," said the man. "It's perfectly safe for you now."

Tom kept eyeing the door. He turned his body to face it, still holding the Louisville Slugger in his two hands.

"Go on," said the man. "Go back to the monastery."

Tom glanced at him. "What do you mean, 'back'?"

"Just go," the man insisted. "Time is running out. You'll see. It will be all right."

The thunder rolled outside again. Tom let the head of the bat slip from his fingers. He lowered the barrel to the floor, still holding on to the handle. He felt deep misgivings about this—and about the man. Who was he? Why wouldn't he tell him his name? Why did the sight of him make Tom feel afraid? And yet, what choice did he have but to trust him, to do what he said? He couldn't fight the creatures off forever. Maybe the answers really were at the monastery. Marie said so. Why would she lie?

"That's right," said the man on the computer soothingly, as if he were reading Tom's thoughts, answering his silent questions. "That's right. You want this to be over, don't you? You want the answers. I know you do."

He so did! He wanted to solve this puzzle and end this nightmare. He wanted that as much as he'd ever wanted anything in his life. This was like being trapped inside a horror movie. He needed to get out.

He made up his mind. He leaned the Warrior against the wall. He took hold of the dresser. With a grunt of effort, he shoved it back across the floor, removing the blockade from the doorway.

"That's right. Just have courage," said the man in the computer. "Isn't that what your brother would've told you? Have courage."

Tom thought he heard a faint tone of mockery in the man's voice, but he told himself he must be mistaken. He picked up the bat again. He reached out slowly. He unlocked the door. He opened it.

The hall was in shadow. There was a faint mist trailing across the doorway. But there were no monsters—not as far as he could see, at any rate.

Slowly, cautiously, he stepped over the threshold, leaving the bedroom behind him. He stepped out into the hall and stood in the darkness.

Just then there was another lightning flash. The silver-white light shot through the hall—and Tom saw the creatures. The malevolents were waiting for him, a crowd of them in the darkness to his right and his left. Drool was dripping from their eager mouths. Their eyes were bright with hunger.

The man had lied to him—but then Tom had already known that, hadn't he? Deep down, he had known the man was lying all along. He had been so desperate to believe him he had pushed down the knowledge, but it was always there. Now he saw the truth—but it was too late.

The thunder crashed and the beasts rushed at him,

swarmed over him, their claws tearing at him, their teeth ripping into his flesh.

The last thing Tom heard in his agony was the voice of the man on the computer. The man was laughing.

PART II

THE HAUNTED
SCHOOL

11.

Tom cried out in pain and terror—and he opened his eyes.

Immediately, relief flooded through him. The nightmare was over. The monsters were gone.

He was in heaven again, just as before.

Just as before, he was standing on the brink of the vast and peaceful parkland with its stunningly green grass and its blindingly white Greek temples. The sky was a cloudless blue again. The light was golden, and the flower beds planted here and there were more colorful than any he had ever seen.

He looked around him in wonder. What a beautiful place it was! It was as if he had dreamed about it and now he had come here for real. Those monsters in the hallway—the malevolents—they must have killed him. He must be dead now—dead and gone to heaven. That was the only way he could make sense of it.

Some things were different here this time, he noticed. There weren't as many people as there had been before. There were only a few now, a few men and women standing here and there. He particularly noticed this one guy again—the lanky young guy with long dirty blond hair. He was exactly where he'd been the last time. He hadn't moved from his spot in front of one of the temples. His thin, hungry face with its sunken cheeks and darkly ringed eyes was still turning this way and that nervously, as if he were lost and wanted to ask directions but couldn't quite bring himself to do it.

Whatever, Tom thought. The important thing, after being trapped in that horror movie of a house, was how beautiful this place was, how peaceful. No fog. No bizarre voices. No monsters. Maybe the Lying Man in the computer wasn't such a bad guy after all. Maybe the lie he had told to coax Tom out of his room had been well-intentioned. Sure, there had been moments of terror and agony when he'd stepped out into that hall and the malevolents attacked him. But now he was here. In this peaceful place. So maybe the man in the computer was right to lie. Maybe things were going to be okay after all.

Tom took a hesitant step forward. A wonderful thought had come into his mind. It was the same thought that had come to him last time, just before the phone had rung and brought him back to his bedroom. He thought: *If this is heaven, then Burt must be here.* He would be able to see Burt. He would be able to talk to Burt again. Burt would know what was going on. Burt would have the answers.

What would Tom give—what *wouldn't* he give—for the chance to hang out with Burt even one more time?

A smile began to play at the corners of Tom's lips as he started searching the faces of the people in the garden. But at the same time, he became dimly aware of a noise in the background. What was that?

Oh no, Tom thought.

It was his phone! Right on cue. His stupid cell phone was ringing again, playing the guitar riff from the old Merle Haggard song. A sour feeling came into Tom's stomach and rose from there up into his throat. If he turned away from the park . . . if he answered that phone . . . would it take him back? To the nightmare? To the pain? To the horror?

He did not want that to happen. He did not want to go back.

Well, why should he? All he had to do was take one more step, one more, and he would enter this beautiful and peaceful place forever. No more monsters. No more fog and fear. No more suffering. Why would he ever turn back? Why would he ever want to answer that phone?

Behind him, the phone kept ringing, singing insistently. Tom gave a fierce shake of his head, determined to ignore it. He would continue forward. He would walk into the beautiful park. He would find his brother. He and Burt would be together again.

Why was he hesitating?

A memory. A memory from his childhood had sparked and flared in Tom's mind, just a flash, there and gone in a single instant. Such a strange, random thing to think about. Why had it come to him? And why did it make him pause?

He had remembered how three of Burt's friends came to the house once for a sleepover a long time ago. Tom was just a little boy then, five or six. He was supposed to go upstairs to bed early. But he begged his mom to let him hang out with the big kids. Mom said he could stay up with them for a little while if it was okay with Burt. And Burt said it was okay.

This was before Tom and Burt had redone the basement. The best TV they had was in the back room then.

Tom was thrilled to sit there cross-legged on the rug and watch the movie *Tuck Everlasting* with the big kids. He didn't say much. He was afraid Burt's friends would make fun of him if he did. He just sat and listened to the big-kid talk and watched the show.

After a while, Burt had gotten up and gone into the kitchen to make some popcorn. While he was gone, one of his friends—Vince Lindstrom, his name was—had started talking to Tom.

"Hey, did you hear about the guy with the hook?" Vince asked him.

Tom had not heard about the guy with the hook. Vince began to tell him. He told him that there was a man roaming around Springland who had a big hook where his right hand should have been. Vince said the hook guy crept into kids' bedrooms at night, hooked them around the neck, and stole them away.

"It's a true story," Vince said.

Tom didn't really believe Vince, but he sort of did believe him at the same time. Anyway, he started to get scared—really scared that he might go to bed and the hook guy would come into his room and steal him.

Finally, Burt came back with the popcorn.

"Hey, Burt," said Vince, with a big grin. "I've been telling your brother all about the hook."

Burt carefully set the bowl of popcorn down on the table by the sofa. Then he walked over and gave Vince a slap on the back of the head. It was a friendly slap—but not that friendly. Hard enough—*whack!*—so that Vince cried out.

"Ow! Hey! What's that for?"

"Don't lie to him," said Burt.

"Aw, I was just giving him a hard time," said Vince, rubbing the spot on his head where Burt had thwacked him.

"You can give him a hard time all you want. You can tease him. You can make fun of him. He's my little brother. That's what he's here for. But don't ever lie to him. It's not allowed."

Even though he was just a little kid, Tom had somehow understood this—understood why Burt made this rule. He and Burt didn't have a father. Their father had left before Tom was born. Tom had never even seen the man. Mom was a great mom. She worked hard to pay for their house and for food and everything. She was an assistant at a law firm—a paralegal—and sometimes she had to stay up with her papers long into the night to get all her work done. But she still found time to be Mom, to make breakfast, to make sure her sons got to school, to help them with their homework and all that. There was nothing wrong with Mom, it was just . . .

It was just that without a father, Tom felt that there was

no one in his life who would tell him the truth, no matter what. There were just some things Mom wouldn't say to him, some things she was too nice to say or too embarrassed to say. She would never say, for instance, *You are acting like a complete and total idiot,* even if he was. She would never say, *If that bully bothers you again, slug him one in the cake-hole.* She would never tell him what girls were really thinking about. Stuff like that.

But Burt would tell him those things. No matter what the subject was, no matter what the problem was, Burt would tell it to him straight, as much as he knew and as much as he thought Tom could understand. It wasn't that Burt was always right. Sometimes he didn't know the answers. Sometimes he got the answers wrong. But Tom knew Burt would never lie to him intentionally, never say anything he didn't believe. That was the rule.

And that was the memory that came back to Tom as he stood hesitating on the border of the garden, as he stood looking out over the green grass and the bright flowers and the majestic Greek temples. He heard the phone ringing behind him, ringing and ringing, threatening to draw him back into a world of pain and fear.

Why had he remembered that night of the sleepover? Why did it make him hesitate to step into the garden?

The answer came to him.

No matter how peaceful this garden seemed, he was here because the man in the computer had lied to him, had tricked him, had talked him into going back out into the hall where the malevolent monsters were waiting.

But Burt—Burt had told him to fight. Burt's voice had shouted to him from the television set, telling him not to give in to the monsters, not to despair—that despair was never an option. Burt had urged him to find the baseball bat—the Warrior—and make a stand against the creatures who wanted to destroy him.

And Burt never lied.

Tom gazed longingly at this mysterious parkland that seemed to him like heaven. His heart yearned for its beauty and its peace. The phone ringing insistently behind him sounded irritating and discordant. He knew that if he turned back to answer it, he would step right back into a nightmare.

But he knew—he knew in his heart—that Burt would want him to go back. Go back and fight—go back and figure out what was going on—get to the bottom of things, get to the truth of the matter.

Tom was a reporter, after all. Finding the truth was his business. Finding the truth—even when it was painful, even when it went against his own inclinations and desires. Even when it made everyone in school hate him.

He took one last yearning look around him. The green

lawn. The white temples. The golden light. He wanted to go into the park. He wanted to go to heaven.

But he heard the phone singing its song in the distance behind him. He summoned all the willpower he had and turned back to answer it.

12.

Tom blinked, confused. Where was he?

He looked around him. His eyes passed over the framed newspaper stories, the sports pennants, the long flag from Burt's coffin. He was in his bedroom at home.

A dream, he thought. *Heaven was a dream.*

He heard the guitar riff, the Haggard song, his phone ringing. He twisted until he could see the phone on his computer table. It jumped and rattled around as it rang.

A dream, he thought again. *It was all just . . .*

No. Wait. He sat up in bed quickly, tossing the comforter aside. He remembered. The heavenly park. This empty house. The fog outside. The monsters.

This was no dream. This was real—bizarre but totally real. And it was all happening again!

He reached out quickly and grabbed the phone. Checked the readout to see who was calling.

Number blocked.

Right. Just like before. He remembered that, too. The phone vibrated in his hand as it rang again. He answered.

He knew what he would hear before he heard it. There it was. That static. Weird white noise coming from an alien and frightening place far away. He listened intently. Next there would be a voice. The voice of that ghostly woman in the white blouse . . .

It began, "I need to talk to you. It's important."

He could hear her a little better this time, a little more clearly than he'd heard her before.

"Where are you?" he said, trying to keep his own voice steady and clear. "I need to find you. I need to know where you are."

"My address is . . ." Then the static overwhelmed her. Her voice was swept under the crackle and hiss.

"What's your address?" Tom shouted. "Say it again."

The woman tried again, calling to him from beneath the static. Her voice was now so dim that Tom's face contorted with the effort to make out her words.

"... school ... you left my address ..."

"At school?" Tom said, straining to hear her. "I left your address at school?"

Yes. That was right. He wasn't sure how he knew, but he knew. Her address was at the office of the *Sentinel*. He had scribbled it on a pad there.

"Please ... please ... you have to ...," the woman called to him—and then, as he knew they would, the two beeps came. He pulled the phone away from his ear and looked at the readout.

Connection lost.

This time Tom didn't hesitate. He leapt out of bed. He rushed to his dresser. He pulled on his sweatpants and the Tigers sweatshirt as fast as he could.

A familiar feeling of excitement was coursing through him: the feeling he got when a news story began to come together, when things began to make sense. This was what he loved about working on the *Sentinel*: finding the answers. And he was beginning to find them now. He was beginning to figure this crazy thing out, beginning to understand what was happening.

And he knew what he had to do next.

He didn't bother to stop in the bathroom this time. It didn't matter whether he shaved or not. None of that ordinary stuff mattered anymore. He just had to get to the basement as fast as he could. It was a matter of life and death.

He stampeded down the stairs into the front hall. He paused at the door only a moment to look out through the sidelight. The lawn and the driveway were clear again. No fog. He could see all the way down to the end of the driveway. The newspaper was lying there near the street, just as it had been the first time. And the mist was beginning to gather in the street as it had before, too. Soon, he knew, the fog would move in. It would become thick again. And it would bring the malevolents with it.

He didn't have a lot of time. He had to hurry.

He ran down the hall to the kitchen, to the basement door. As he pulled the door open, he half expected to hear Burt's voice again, shouting from the TV screen.

This is your mission!

But no. It was different this time. The basement was silent. Tom understood. Burt had called to him before because he wanted to get him to come down, to see what was on television, to face a truth his mind didn't want to face. Burt had reached out to him from an impossible distance and done the best he could to get his message across the gulf between them.

But this time Tom didn't need that help. This time he was ready to face the truth on his own. He was scared—he was very scared—but he was ready.

He went down the stairs.

He came into the family room. Saw the TV with its dark screen. The silent speakers. Fighting down the anxiety that tightened his throat, he moved to the easy chairs. There was the remote lying on the seat of the nearest chair. He picked it up. Pointed it at the TV. Pressed the Power button.

It was time to face the facts.

For a moment, the TV stayed dark. The silence went on for such a long time that Tom began to think he had gotten it wrong, that he would have to look for the truth elsewhere. Another silent second passed, and then another. Tom started to turn away.

Then a voice startled him by shouting over the speakers, "Dr. Leonard to the ER—stat!"

There it was. Just like before. Only different. The voice was calling for Dr. Leonard this time, not Dr. Cooper. Tom got it. Dr. Cooper was just a character in the TV show Mom liked. Dr. Leonard was real. Tom had seen *The Cooper Practice* on the screen before because he wasn't ready to face reality. Now he was. At least he hoped he was.

The TV came on. The nurses and aides and doctors were

crowding around the gurney as they rolled it up the corridor to the emergency operating room.

"Single GSW to the chest!"

"His pulse is falling fast!"

"Clear Trauma One."

They rolled the gurney down the hall and came to an alcove hidden behind a curtain. One of the aides tore the curtain aside, and the gurney was rushed through into the emergency operating room.

"Where's Dr. Leonard?"

"Here I am. What have we got?"

"Single GSW to the chest. We're losing him."

"Get him onto the operating table. On my count of three."

The people around the gurney leaned in as the doctor counted off.

"One, two—three."

Tom's pulse sped up as he watched them lift the body—the body hidden behind their bodies—from the gurney onto the operating table. He knew what was going to happen next, of course. He knew what he was going to see.

The crowd around the operating table broke apart—and there he was. Tom stood in the basement and stared helplessly as he saw himself on the television set. He saw himself lying unconscious on the operating table, his torso covered in blood. The doctors and nurses darted here and there around him. One nurse sliced Tom's shirt off with a small knife, and another began to clean his wound. A third worked a tube into his throat so he would be able to breathe. Once again it made Tom gag as he stood there watching it happen on the screen. He felt his legs go weak beneath him as he watched. He sank down slowly into the easy chair behind him. Leaning forward on the edge of his seat, he went on staring at the scene.

But the next moment was so difficult for him to watch that he had to narrow his eyes until they were almost shut—make the images less clear, less devastating. Even so, he could hardly bear the sight of the doctor laying the blade of the scalpel against his bare skin. He let out a groan as he watched the blade slice into his flesh, the red blood flowing out from underneath the flashing steel.

Sitting in the armchair, Tom flinched with pain. He bent forward and grabbed his chest. It was as if he could actually feel them cutting him open, could feel them tearing his flesh apart to get at the bullet lodged inside him. The scene on the television set—the television set itself—the basement family room—everything—seemed to tumble and spin around him. Reality seemed to retreat into murky darkness. Tom felt himself fading away until his consciousness became a dwindling point of light surrounded by a vaster and vaster emptiness—an emptiness like space itself.

He blinked and shook his head fiercely, fighting his way back to full awareness. He forced himself to stare through the murk of his mind, to see the TV clearly again. Even if it meant he had to watch himself being cut open, he had to know what had happened. He had to know the truth.

But now—thankfully!—he saw that the scene had changed. The operating room was gone. Tom saw himself lying in a bed now. A number of tubes ran out of his body, out of his arm and out from under the blankets. Fluid dripped into him from a bag of some sort. A monitor was beeping by his head. A respirator was pumping air into him. He was lying in a hospital room now. Unconscious. Still.

The camera slowly drew back so that Tom could see more of the room. He saw a small wooden chair beside his bed. He saw a woman sitting there.

As he watched, Tom let out a soft groan of surprise and pain and longing.

The woman in the chair was his mom.

The sight of his mother sitting in the hospital room beside him made Tom's heart feel tight and small. She was sitting bent forward, her head bowed, her elbows on her knees, her hands clasped in front of her as if she was in prayer. She was rocking herself back and forth, back and forth at the edge of the mattress on which Tom lay motionless. She wasn't crying, but when she raised her eyes to look at her unconscious son, the expression on her face was awful to see. It was a look of such wasted grief that Tom wanted to jam his hand through the television screen so he could touch her, comfort her. He hadn't seen his mom look so bad since . . . well, since the army officers had come to tell her that Burt had been killed in action. He wanted to call out to her, to say, *I'm here, Mom. I'm not that figure on the bed. I'm right here.*

But he didn't. He knew she wouldn't hear him. She was there, in that reality. And he was here, in this one.

So he just sat there, watching helplessly—which was so painful to him that he felt a powerful urge to close his eyes and turn away. But he understood that if he did that, the television would turn itself off. That's what had happened before. The scenes on TV were just projections from his own mind. The set had gone dark before because he hadn't been ready to face the whole truth. If he refused to face it now, there would be darkness again and he didn't know if the TV would ever come back on.

He had to force himself to go on watching. It was like forcing himself to ask a source difficult questions during an interview. It could be awkward, even painful, but sometimes he had to do it. The only difference now was that he was the source—the source as well as the reporter. Watching the TV was like interviewing his own brain. He had to force himself to want the truth more than he wanted to escape the pain of knowing.

Whatever happens, he thought, *whatever the truth turns out to be, it's better to know than not to know. There's no other way to live.*

So he leaned forward in his chair and concentrated as hard as he could. He suffered through the pain of watching his mother as she wrung her hands and rocked herself, as she stared at him where he lay on the bed motionless as a corpse.

Now a new figure entered the scene. It was a man in blue scrubs—those pajama-like outfits doctors wear. He was a man in his thirties with black hair. He had bland features and pale, almost pasty skin. He wore glasses with heavy frames and blinked rapidly behind them, which made him look very young and sort of helpless. Tom knew some-how that this was the surgeon who had cut him open: Dr. Leonard.

Tom's mother got quickly to her feet. Tom's throat grew tight as he saw the look of terror deep in her eyes. She searched the doctor's face for news, trying to guess what he was going to say before he said it.

"Mrs. Harding?" the doctor said.

"Yes," Mom answered. Her voice was hoarse, almost a

whisper. "What's happening to my son? Is he going to be all right? Is he going to . . . ?"

She couldn't say the word—the word *die*. But Tom knew that's what she was asking. She went on searching the doctor's face for the answer. And Tom stared at the scene on the television, waiting for the answer, too. *Was* he going to die? Was that what was happening to him? Was that why nothing made sense around him? Was he dying—or already dead and in some limbo waiting for God to decide whether he should go to heaven or hell? Marie had told him no, he wasn't dead, but maybe she had gotten it wrong. Maybe . . .

"Your son is alive, but . . . ," Dr. Leonard said. He hesitated, and Tom's mother reached out convulsively and gripped his arm.

"But what? Tell me."

"He's lost a lot of blood," the doctor went on, "and I'm afraid he's fallen into a coma."

For a second, Tom's mother seemed unable to understand. She slowly shook her head, narrowing her eyes.

"A coma? I don't . . . For how long? Will he come back? Will he wake up?"

"I don't know," said Dr. Leonard. "Mrs. Harding, please sit down."

He gestured toward her chair. Mrs. Harding sank back into it. The doctor pulled up another chair and sat down beside her. Her eyes never left his face. She went on staring at him, openmouthed.

"Mrs. Harding," Dr. Leonard went on gently. "Your son was wounded very badly. The bullet nicked his superior vena cava—one of his major blood vessels—and punctured his lung . . ."

Tom's mother made an awful noise and covered her mouth with both hands.

"While he was on the operating table," Dr. Leonard said, "his heart stopped . . ."

Tom's mother lowered her hands and said, "You mean he died?"

"Well," said the doctor, "I suppose you could put it like that, yes. Yes, he did. We were able to revive him, but . . . well, until he regains consciousness, we won't know very much about how he is or how much damage he suffered."

"Damage?" Tom's mother said. "You mean . . ."

"Brain damage."

Sitting in the chair, watching the scene on the television, Tom groaned aloud. His mother began to cry.

The doctor tried to reassure her, touching her shoulder. "We just don't know. We can't tell yet. He may come out of this in an hour. And he may be totally fine. Or . . ."

"Or he may never come out of it," Mom said through her tears. "He may die."

Dr. Leonard nodded. "We can't promise you anything.

We just don't know. Unless or until he comes around, there's not that much I can tell you."

Tom's mother couldn't take any more. She turned away from the doctor. She reached out and took Tom's hand where it lay limp atop the bedcover. She brought the hand to her lips and kissed it and she began to weep. "My boys," she said, her voice muffled by tears. "Both my boys!"

The doctor stood up silently and walked out. As he did, Tom saw for the first time that there was another bed in the room. Another man was lying in the second bed, hooked up to a bunch of tubes like Tom, unconscious like Tom. As his mother sobbed beside him, Tom stared at this other man in the other bed.

"What?" he said aloud.

Shocked, he realized he recognized the man in the bed. It was the lanky young man with dirty blond hair, the man he had seen in the heavenly garden looking lost and afraid. Tom saw that both the man's wrists were bandaged.

Tom shut his eyes. It was too much. His mother in such an agony of sorrow. The man from the heavenly park in the hospital room. He couldn't understand it all. He couldn't bear to think about it anymore. He looked away—and instantly, the TV snapped off and went blank.

In the silence of the basement room, Tom put a trembling hand to his forehead. He closed his eyes. For a long moment, he couldn't think at all. He just sat there, his mind empty of everything—everything except confusion and the image of his mom weeping over him—and the pain and sorrow he felt for her.

Then he lowered his hand and his shoulders slumped. Well, now he had what he wanted. Now he knew the truth.

He looked at the TV. At the blank screen. He thought: *Help me, dude. Help me.* He was trying to reach Burt somehow, trying to get Burt to come back on the screen, to talk to him, to tell him what he should do, how he could get himself out of this.

The TV remained silent, the screen blank.

Tom raised his eyes to the ceiling—to heaven. Soon, he knew, the fog would roll in again. Soon the monsters would burst through the windows again. This time there would be no escape. This time there would be no survival. He could not leave his mother in that hospital room all alone with his dead body. Her heart was already broken because of losing Burt. Losing him too would destroy her.

He had to find a way back to her, back to consciousness and life. But how? For the moment, Tom was all out of answers.

Please help me, God, he thought. *I so totally don't know what to do. Please.*

He lowered his eyes to the TV again. But still: nothing. Silence.

Then he nearly jumped to his feet as he heard a loud noise upstairs.

Someone—or something—was pounding on the front door.

13.

The mist in the driveway had thickened. The figure standing in the mist looked like Death.

Tom had come running up from the basement as soon as he'd heard the pounding on the door. But even as he crested the stairs, before he even started down the hallway to the foyer, the pounding stopped. Now he was standing at the front door, peering out through the sidelight. He saw the figure who had been knocking. It was retreating, moving slowly down the front path, deeper into the thickening mist.

The figure wore a black raincoat, a black hood. It was a

grim and ominous sight that made Tom's stomach go sour with fear.

Like Death.

The ghostly figure glided slowly away from him, toward the deeper mist already gathering at the bottom of the driveway. Soon, Tom knew, the figure would vanish into the marine layer, the same way the woman in the white blouse had vanished the last time.

And yet Tom did not move from where he was. He did not open the door. He didn't call out. He wasn't sure whether he should. The cowled figure was so frightening to look at that he was afraid if he called to it—if it turned—it might actually present the skeletal face of the Grim Reaper. Would it come to him then and claim him and carry him away to his own grave?

Tom thought about it one more second while the cowled figure continued to move down the walk, growing hazier and dimmer as the mist collected around it.

Then he made up his mind. He had come back to this house to find the truth. He would find it, even if it wore the face of Death itself.

He pulled the door open. He stepped out across the threshold.

"Wait!" he called, his voice trembling.

The hooded figure stopped, stood still. The mist on the front lawn blew and swirled and grew denser and the figure grew more vague, more ghostly. A shiver of cold and fear went through Tom as he felt the damp of the mist touch his skin. He suddenly felt very vulnerable. He knew the malevolents were out here, moving in the fog, not far away, getting closer every moment.

He forced himself to speak. "Who are you?"

Slowly, the figure began to turn around. It faced him. Its features were obscured in the shadow of the hood.

Tom held his breath. He thought: *Is this it? Is this Death? Is this the end?*

Then the figure lifted a hand—a small white hand. It pushed the hood back. A mass of red hair tumbled free, framing a pug-nosed, freckled face. Green eyes blinked at him from behind the round lenses of a pair of glasses.

It was Lisa McKay.

Tom let out a breath of sweet relief as Lisa broke out into a tremulous smile.

"Thank heavens!" she said. "I was afraid you were already gone!"

INTERLUDE TWO

"Sources: Tiger Champs Used Drugs."

In the days after the story broke, Tom's life was like a

thunderstorm: long periods of gloom and turmoil and darkness punctuated by sudden shafts of dazzling light. There were the glowering looks in the school halls every day; black, angry looks in class even from his friends, even from some of his teachers. There were whispers as he walked the halls: "Traitor." "Creep." "Liar." There were hard shots from the shoulders of some of the bigger guys as they passed him. Every morning he awoke with dread, walked to school with dread, knowing he was going to face it all again. Long, gloomy, stormy hours. And then suddenly . . .

Suddenly, Marie. Marie's eyes; Marie's lips; Marie's voice, a gentle whisper. Her golden hair spilling around a face like a porcelain doll's. She sought him out on the playing field after lunch. She sat with him under the oak tree during study period. She let him drive her home. She sat in the car with him and put her hand in his.

He could not believe it was happening. It was as if his daydreams had sprung to life.

"Won't everyone hate you?" he asked her. They were sitting together on a windowsill early one morning, just before the homeroom bell rang. "For hanging out with me, I mean."

"I don't care what everyone thinks," she told him. "And neither should you."

"What about . . . ?" He didn't want to ask, but he couldn't help himself. "What about Gordon? I always thought . . . Well, everyone always thought you were with Gordon."

"Like I said," she answered softly, leaning toward him. "I don't care what everyone thinks. I want you to come to my house next week, Tom. Daddy wants to meet you."

Her face was so close to his just then that he felt breathless. "Really?" he said.

But before Marie could answer, the moment was shattered.

"Tom."

Tom blinked. Looked up from Marie as if coming awake. Miss Dunphy, the principal's assistant, was standing over them. "Mr. Kramer would like to see you in his office," she said. "Right now."

Mr. Kramer, the principal, was waiting for him in the conference room. And not just Mr. Kramer. Coach Petrie was there, too—the Tigers' coach and the head of the Physical Education Department—and so was Mrs. Rafferty, the English teacher who was supposed to supervise the publication of the *Sentinel* but never really did. They were all sitting around the long table, looking at Tom as he entered the room. And the minute Tom saw the expressions on their faces, he knew he was in for big-time trouble.

Mr. Kramer sat at the table's head. He was a young-looking man, in his early forties. He had short white hair, and his eyes were such a pale gray as to be almost colorless. Usually he was a pretty friendly guy, but when the smile disappeared from his face, there was something almost chilling about those transparent eyes of his. There was nothing like a smile on his face now.

He indicated an empty chair and Tom sat down, feeling his stomach jump with anxiety.

Mr. Kramer cleared his throat and shifted in his seat. "We want to talk to you about this story you wrote in the newspaper," he said. "To publicly accuse our football team of taking drugs three years ago—our championship team— that's a very serious charge, you know. We're very proud of our team in this school, Tom."

Tom opened his mouth to answer, but then he jumped in his chair as—*wham!*—Coach Petrie slapped the table loudly. The coach was wearing a short-sleeved polo shirt, and the muscles in his arms tensed and bulged. "It's a lie, that's what it is!" he growled. "You asked me about it and I told you myself it was a lie, didn't I? Didn't I tell you that?"

Mr. Kramer made a calming gesture at him. "Hold on, Coach," he said. Then he went on to Tom, "I think what Coach is trying to say is that we're disappointed you went ahead and wrote the story even after he explained to you that there was no truth in it. That's irresponsible, Tom."

Tom drew a breath, hoping he could keep his voice

steady. "I quoted Coach in the story," he said. "I gave him a chance to tell his side of it."

"Yeah, and then you made me sound like some kind of liar," Coach Petrie snapped back.

Tom felt a cold sweat break out on the back of his neck. This was bad, really bad. Three adults—three powerful adults—angry at him. No, furious. Coach Petrie looked like he wanted to wring his neck.

He forced himself to return their glares with a steady gaze. "The story wasn't irresponsible," he said. "My sources gave me proof of everything they told me. Cell phone pictures. E-mails. Personal testimonies from players who took the steroids. It's all in the paper and I checked it all myself. The story was solid. The players took drugs. We won the championship unfairly. Those are the facts."

Tom recoiled—he couldn't help it—as Coach pointed a finger right in his face. "You are calling me a liar, aren't you? How dare you disrespect me? Who do you think you are?"

"I'm just saying it's the truth," said Tom as steadily as he could. He wished he were somewhere else right now. Somewhere like Mars.

"You're supposed to run all stories by me for approval," Mrs. Rafferty broke in, her voice clipped and hard. She was a large, pasty-faced woman with short red hair that curled up out of her head like fire. "I would never have approved the newspaper running a story like this."

Tom knew that Lisa always e-mailed the paper to Mrs. Rafferty for approval—and that Mrs. Rafferty never read it and never responded. But he hadn't personally seen Lisa send the e-mail this time, and he didn't want to sound like he was blaming Lisa for anything, so he kept his mouth shut.

"All right," said Mr. Kramer, making another conciliatory gesture at the others. "Let's not waste time with anger and recriminations. Let's see if we can make this right. Tom, if we let this story stand, it's going to have serious repercussions. The school board is going to ask questions, the interscholastic sports governors, maybe even the state Board of Ed. I'm going to need to have as much information as I can in order to answer them and explain how this rumor got started and how it got out of hand like this. To begin with, I need to know who told you these tales about the team."

The sweat gathering on Tom's neck rolled down his back, making his shirt damp. "I can't tell you that," he said. "My sources gave me this information on the condition I keep their names secret. I promised them I would."

Tom started as Coach Petrie slapped the table again. "Well, you are going to break that promise, son, believe you me," he said.

"I don't think you understand the situation you're in," said Mrs. Rafferty—and the way she said it made Tom feel that her hair was going to catch fire for real. "You are facing suspension here."

Tom's mouth went dry. Suspension! That was not good. That was bad, in fact. It would go on his record. It would hurt his chances of getting into a top college. Worse than that: he didn't know how he would tell his mom.

But he knew he had no choice about this. He licked his lips. He said, "The people who talked to me wouldn't have talked if they thought they were going to be named—they were afraid of being punished and attacked for telling the truth." *The way I'm being punished and attacked for telling the truth,* he didn't add. "But they proved what they said beyond a doubt, and I printed the proof. The story is fair and it's true. Even if you suspend me—even if you expel me—it'll still be true."

Mr. Kramer leaned forward, his expression as serious as Tom had ever seen it, his eyes as transparent as glass. "I hope you understand," he said tersely. "Mrs. Rafferty is quite right about this. You are facing very serious consequences here."

Tom took a deep, unsteady breath. "I do understand," he said softly. "But I stand by the story. I stand by the story."

Tom had to say it twice to get the words out clearly—and

even though he meant them, he quailed inside as he saw the anger flash in Mr. Kramer's colorless eyes.

Mrs. Rafferty started to say, "You do not know the beginning of how much trouble you are getting yourself—"

But she stopped as there was a quick knock on the door. Before anyone could say anything else, the door opened and Lisa came in.

She was wearing jeans and a striped pullover and tennis shoes. Her red hair tumbled messily down the sides of her pale face, and she blinked rapidly behind her glasses. She looked very small and skinny and much younger than she was.

"Hi, everyone!" she said in a chirpy little-girl voice. "I heard you guys were talking to Tom and I thought, since I'm the newspaper editor, maybe I should be here, too."

"We'll speak to you separately," said Mr. Kramer tersely.

"And you're not the editor anymore," growled Mrs. Rafferty.

"Oh!" said Lisa, as if she were startled. "Really? Is this about the Tigers story?"

"It sure is!" said Coach Petrie.

"Okay," said Lisa in that same high, bright voice. "I'm sort of surprised to hear that, because I did send the story to you for approval, Mrs. Rafferty."

"Well, I didn't approve it," she snapped.

"Well, yes, I know, but you haven't approved any of our stories since I've been on the paper. We always send them to you, but you never get back to us. So, you know, I didn't think this was any different. Anyway . . . ," she went on chirpily, "let me know when you're done with Tom. Because when *USA Today* interviews me, they'll probably want him there, too."

Mr. Kramer, Coach Petrie, and Mrs. Rafferty all sat up straight at the same time and said exactly the same thing: "What?!"

"*USA Today,*" Lisa repeated with the same cheery tone. "You know, for their story about us and the Tigers and how a school paper got a big scoop and how the school reacted to it and all that."

Mr. Kramer's eyes flashed again. He seemed as if he was about to slap the table himself. "I absolutely forbid you to talk to *USA Today* or anyone else about this until we've fully ascertained the facts!" he said.

And suddenly, Lisa's chirpy, little-girl demeanor vanished—just like that. Her face became very serious, and the eyes behind the round lenses were unblinking and bright as flashing steel. Her voice became flat and hard. "With respect, Mr. Kramer," she said, "I'll be speaking to them after school and with my mother's permission. You don't have the power to forbid me. You have the power to take me and Tom off the paper. You have the power to suspend us. You have the power to close the paper down. But we told the truth and we're going to go on telling it, in *USA Today* and on Facebook and Twitter and wherever else we can to whoever will listen. And I know that'll be okay with you," she said, turning her steady gaze from one adult to another. "Because as long as you do what's right, you won't mind if everyone knows."

With that, she turned and walked out of the room.

A few minutes later Tom found her in the *Sentinel*'s office.

"You saved my life in there, Leese," he said with a lopsided smile. "After they heard about *USA Today*, everyone suddenly got a lot more friendly. I guess they didn't want the whole country to find out they were trying to cover up for the team."

Lisa shrugged but blushed at the same time. "That's what friends are for, Tommy. I knew you could stand up for yourself, but I figured, I'm the editor, it's my responsibility to protect the story."

Weary with relief, Tom dropped into his chair and put his feet up on the mess on his desk. "So when do we talk to *USA Today*?" he asked her.

Lisa shrugged her narrow shoulders. "I don't know. They haven't asked us yet."

Tom's feet dropped off the desk with a *thud* as he came rocketing upright in his chair. "What?"

"Well, I had to say something, right? They looked like they were about to hang you."

"So you lied?"

"I didn't lie. I said when *USA Today* interviews me, they'll probably want to interview you, too. I'm sure that's true."

"Lisa!"

"Well, let's call it a bluff," she said.

Tom fell back against his chair, staring at her with his mouth open. After another moment, he laughed.

"What's so funny?" she asked him.

"Nothing," said Tom. "Just remind me never to play poker with you!"

Lisa's cheeks turned so red her freckles all but disappeared. A moment later she was giggling helplessly.

14.

urry!" Tom said to her now. "We don't have much
time."

He took ahold of Lisa's elbow as she stepped into
the house. Before he shut the door behind her, he cast one
last look outside, across the front lawn. Sheets and tendrils
of mist were coiling up the drive and over the grass, casting a
ghostly pall over everything. At the bottom of the driveway,
the fog was gathering quickly. As Tom stood staring through

the cloudy air, he thought he saw a shadow move in that thicker whiteness. A malevolent. Waiting for the moment when it could reach the house; reach him. Soon.

Tom shut the door.

"Come on," he said.

He drew Lisa down the hallway to the kitchen. They sat face-to-face at the round table in the nook, just as he'd sat with Marie. Outside, through the windows, a faint mist had begun to gather over the backyard as well. Tom knew it would get thicker quickly. The malevolents were on their way.

Still gripping her elbow, Tom leaned toward Lisa. She had opened her raincoat now. Beneath it, she was wearing the pink blouse he knew was her favorite. The top button was undone, and a gold necklace with a little gold cross shone against the white skin of her throat. Tom could not believe how good it was to see that quirky, freckled, pug-nosed face of hers. He felt certain she would be able to help him find the truth. She always had.

"I was shot, wasn't I?" he asked her. "That's why I'm here. Someone shot me in the chest."

Lisa nodded quickly. She wasn't smiling anymore. She looked serious, pale, worried. "That's right."

"Who was it? Who did it, Leese?"

"I don't know. No one knows. The police are still trying to find out."

"But it must've been someone who was angry at me about our story, right? Someone who was angry because of what I wrote about the Tigers."

"Probably. That's what everyone thinks, anyway."

"I should know who it is!" he said. "But I don't remember."

"Well, you're hurt."

"Right. I'm in a coma, aren't I?"

"Yes."

"I'm lying unconscious in the hospital, and the doctors can't wake me up."

Lisa frowned, her eyes growing damp. "Yes, that's right. It's awful. We're all so frightened."

Tom tried to take this in, to think it through. He was still holding loosely on to Lisa's arm. Lisa moved her hand to his. Her cool touch was comforting.

"And so all this," he said, gesturing at the kitchen. "All this is happening in my mind, in my imagination."

Lisa tilted her head, her expression uncertain. "Well . . . yes . . . but . . ."

"But what?" said Tom. He could feel the time passing, could feel the fog moving in. He knew that every second counted. "Tell me. Don't hold anything back."

"Well . . . just because something is in your imagination doesn't mean it's imaginary."

Tom shook his head. "I don't get it."

"Your imagination isn't just some kind of fantasyland or something. It's a way of seeing things that your rational mind can't see or doesn't want to see. It's a way of knowing things you can't know any other way. The things you see with your imagination may not look like the things you see in ordinary life, but they're just as real in their own way. And all this—everything that's happening here, Tom—*it's all real.* And it's serious. It's like . . . It's like your imagination is the battleground on which you're fighting for your life."

"Right," said Tom, trying to stay with her, trying to understand. "The fog, the monsters, the malevolents . . ."

"They can kill you—really kill you. They already *have* killed you. Twice! Your heart has already stopped beating two times."

Tom nodded. "Yes. I know. I died. I even saw heaven, I think."

"Well," said Lisa, looking uncertain again, "I don't think it could have been heaven. Not exactly. Not the real heaven. This is your imagination, remember—and I think heaven is probably beyond anything you could imagine."

"But if I died, maybe I saw it for a second . . . ," Tom started to say. His voice trailed away as he remembered the things he had seen in the park, the strangely unhappy-looking people.

"Maybe," said Lisa. "It's possible." She smiled. "But, like

I said, I don't think so. The road to heaven isn't death, Tom. It's life."

Tom went on thinking about it. He went on thinking about the beautiful parkland with the Greek temples and about the people he'd seen there—the people who weren't serene and happy the way you'd think they would be if they were in paradise.

"There was a guy there," he murmured. "A thin guy with long blond hair. I think he's in the hospital with me. I think he's the guy lying unconscious in the bed next to mine."

"Yeah," said Lisa. "The doctor said he was some kind of drug addict, hooked on meth or something. He couldn't take it anymore. He tried to slash his wrists, to kill himself. They don't know whether he's going to make it."

Tom thought about the long-haired guy standing in front of the temple, how he looked lost, like he was trying to find someone who could give him directions. So Lisa was right. The parkland wasn't heaven. Even though Tom's heart had stopped, the place he had seen was still some part of his living mind. If he really died, then there would be something else, something more. Something, as Lisa said, beyond his imagination.

Tom glanced away from the anxious expression on Lisa's face. He glanced out the window into the backyard. Already the mist was noticeably thicker out there. He could see it wafting in, blowing in, more and more of it every second. Soon it would be thick enough to bring the malevolents. Very soon.

He faced Lisa again. "What about you?" he said. "Are you real?"

"You know I am, Tommy."

He smiled, in spite of his worry and fear. *Tommy.* Lisa was the only one who ever called him that. And she only did it when she was emotional, when she forgot to control herself and call him Tom like everyone else did. "But I mean . . . are you really here now?" he asked her. "Really here with me?"

"I'm sitting beside your hospital bed. I'm holding your hand just like this. I'm talking to you. The doctors said that if I talked to you, you might be able to hear me."

"I do hear you," he said. "I mean . . . I don't think . . . I don't think this is what you're really saying exactly. I think a lot of this conversation is me talking to myself in my own mind. But I hear the sound of your voice and . . . I can feel you're there. And I'm glad you're there, Lisa. You've always been a good friend."

Lisa tried to smile, but her mouth trembled down quickly in a deep frown. The lenses of her glasses grew misty. And a thought flashed through Tom's mind, a new thought, one he'd never had before. It was a thought he could barely believe, but there it was anyway. He thought that maybe Lisa liked him—really liked him, not just as a friend, but as more than that. Funny, all that time they'd spent together in the *Sentinel's* office, and he'd never noticed it before. Until this moment, he'd been thinking about Marie so much, yearning for Marie so much, that it never crossed his mind.

Lisa's grip tightened on his hand. "Tom," she said softly. "Listen to me. The doctors say . . ."

She faltered. He answered her grip with his own. "Go on."

"The doctors say if they lose you again, if your heart stops beating again, they doubt they'll be able to revive you. They doubt you'll be strong enough to make it back. And you've got to make it back, Tommy! You've got to. I don't think I could . . . I don't think your mother could survive if she lost you like she lost Burt."

"Right. Right." Tom took a deep breath, braced himself. "What are my chances?" he asked her. "Did the doctors say? What are the chances I'll come out of this coma alive?"

"They said . . ." Lisa's voice broke. A single tear spilled from behind her misted lenses, rolled down her freckled cheek. "They said they didn't know. They said it was fifty-fifty. It could go either way."

Tom made a noise: *whew.* "Fifty-fifty," he repeated. "And if I die again, I'm done for. So I only have one more chance, and if the malevolents get me this time . . ."

Lisa only nodded, unable to speak.

Tom swallowed hard. "Fifty-fifty. One chance. Live or die. Man, that's scary. I'm scared, Lisa. I'm seventeen. I'm not ready to die. But I don't know if I've got the courage to . . ."

"Shh! Shh!" She put a finger to his lips, silencing him. Then she pulled her hand away to wipe her cheek dry. "You have plenty of courage. All you need. More."

"I don't know, I don't know," said Tom. "I was never the hero type. Not like Burt."

"Yes, you are," Lisa told him, crying harder. "You're just as brave as Burt ever was. Just in a different way, that's all. That's . . ." She couldn't finish. She bowed her head.

Tom looked at her, looked at the top of her head, the part in her hair where a line of white scalp peeked through the wavy red. He didn't know why, but the sight of it made her seem fragile to him somehow. Which was funny, seeing as he was the one in the coma, on the brink of death! But he was sorry now that he'd shown her his fear, sorry he'd made her cry. Even if she couldn't really see it sitting there in the hospital next to his bed, he wanted to give her strength, to send his strength to her, his courage to her.

"Okay," he said. "Okay. Fifty-fifty. It's better than nothing, right? I'll take my chances. But what do I do? How do I find my way out of here? How do I get out of this coma and get back to you?"

It was a long moment before Lisa could lift her head, could speak again. Then she said, "I'm not sure, but I can tell you what I think."

Tom knew that the information she was giving him was really information coming from the depths of his own mind. But he needed to hear it. He needed to hear it spoken out loud. He said, "Go on."

"I think there's something holding you here, something that won't let you leave."

"Okay. Like what?"

"I don't know. Believe me, if I knew I would tell you. But there's something, something that wants to keep you in the dark, that wants to keep you in this coma, that maybe even . . . even wants you to die."

"Whoa." He swallowed hard. "Whoa," he said again. "How do I find it, then? How do I get rid of it?"

"Well, whatever it is," Lisa said, "it must be here somewhere. It must be something inside your own mind. Something you know but can't get to somehow."

"You mean, like, something I've forgotten. Or something I'm blocking out."

"That's right. I think . . . ," Lisa went on—and Tom could tell she was working it out as she spoke. "I think maybe if you could find out what happened to you, find out who shot you—who shot you and why—then you could break the barrier, break through and face the truth and wake up."

Her damp eyes gazed into his with so much feeling that Tom looked away, embarrassed. He looked down at the table.

"That's got to be it, Tom," Lisa said. "Find the truth. The truth is always the way, even when it's scary, even when it's hard. It's like the Bible says, you know. Find the truth—and the truth will set you free."

Tom felt a fresh energy go through him, a fresh fire of inspiration. He raised his eyes to hers. They looked at each other for a long moment, and Tom had the strangest feeling that he had never really seen Lisa before. Sure, he'd seen her face. He'd seen her goofy sense of humor and her insecurity about her looks. He'd seen her courage in trying to deal with her parents' divorce and with the fact that she and her mom didn't have much money anymore, even though they used to be rich. He'd seen her—but he'd never seen her like this, never seen the sweet whole of her, the way he was seeing her now, here in his imagination. It was a sight that filled him up in a way he couldn't have described.

Slowly, she drew her hand away from him.

A new bout of fear went through him. "Don't," he whispered before he could stop himself. "Don't leave me."

"I have to, Tom." She stood up. "This isn't something I can do with you." She tried to smile. "I'm just the editor, right? I can send you out on a story, but you've got to find the answers on your own."

He looked up at her. He tried his best to smile. "Man! This imagination—it can be a pretty scary place, you know? I don't want to be alone in here."

"Oh, Tommy," said Lisa. "You're not alone!" Quickly, she reached behind her neck and undid the clasp of her gold necklace. She drew it off her throat and pressed it into his hand. Tom looked down and saw the gold cross gleaming in his palm. "You're not alone, Tommy," Lisa said again. "Just find the truth. And the truth will set you free."

Tom closed his fist around her necklace and held it fast.

The next time he looked up, Lisa was gone.

15.

The moments passed. The house was silent around him. The fog gathered in the backyard. Tom knew his time was running out and yet second after second, he sat where he was, staring at his closed fist.

Find the truth, and the truth will set you free.

All right. Good advice. But how did he do it? How could he find the truth? Where did he begin?

Come on, he told himself. *You're the steely-eyed, big-brained reporter. Figure it out, bro.*

He shook his fist as he went on gazing down at it. To find the whole truth, he needed to know who shot him—who shot him, and why. And hey, how hard could it be to get that information? He had been shot in the chest, after all. The person who shot him must have been standing right in front of him. He must have seen the person at the time it happened. He must already know who it was. So, as Lisa said, the answer must be here somewhere, somewhere inside his mind. But where?

Well, his memory, that's where.

Being in a coma and all, being trapped inside his own imagination, there were obviously things he couldn't remember. So to find those things, somehow he had to get from here, from his imagination, to his memory. But where was that?

Go to the monastery, Tom. That's where the answers are.

He almost heard Marie's gentle voice speak the words. Marie had told him to go to the monastery. That must be the way, and yet . . .

And yet, it didn't make sense to him. The way to his memory should be through the things he remembered. But he didn't remember being in the monastery. He didn't remember that at all.

There was something else, too. The man in the computer. The Lying Man who had told him that the monsters were gone and it was safe to go out into the hall. The Lying Man had told him to go to the monastery, too. The Lying Man had also told him that's where the answers were. Now, okay, maybe the Lying Man had told him the truth about the monastery just to trick him into leaving his bedroom. But Tom had a feeling that the Lying Man never told the truth, not really. Tom had the feeling that everything the Lying Man said was either an outright lie or some other kind of deception.

As he thought about that, an image came into his mind. It was the image of Marie, sitting right here, right in the kitchen, at this very table. He remembered the way she reacted when he wanted to answer his phone. The way she tried to stop him when he wanted to go downstairs to see his brother on TV. Why would she do that? Why would she try to stop him from seeing Burt? Why didn't she want him to answer the phone?

It's not that he didn't trust Marie, he told himself. That would be crazy. Why wouldn't he trust her? It was just that . . . well, he didn't want to do anything the Lying Man told him to do, that's all. That's all.

So where did that leave him?

The seconds passed. He went on sitting there, gripping the necklace, shaking his fist as he thought it through. And a fresh idea came to him. He wanted to get from here to his memory, right? So where was the borderline between the two territories? The border of his memory must be marked by the things he *almost* remembered but couldn't remember completely. If he could find his way to something he *almost* remembered but couldn't quite bring back, then he knew he could find his way from there to the rest of it, the things he had forgotten completely or had blocked out.

What do I almost remember? he asked himself.

The answer came to him at once. The woman in the white blouse. The woman who had called him on the phone and tried to talk to him through the static. She was the one who had called him back from the brink of death, trying to reach him, trying to tell him something. He knew who she was—sort of—but he could not quite place her, could not quite call her identity to mind.

But he knew where to find her, didn't he? He knew where to start at least. She had told him herself.

The office of the *Sentinel* in the basement of the school. He had written her address down on a piece of paper there. That was where the memory trail began. If he could find that address, he could find the woman in the white blouse. If he could find her, he knew somehow that he could find his way back to the rest of it, to everything.

Tom let out a long, unsteady sigh and opened his fist. His hand was empty. Lisa's necklace was gone. He didn't mind. He knew Lisa herself was still there, still nearby, sitting by his bed, praying for him, waiting for him.

You're not alone, Tommy.

He looked up. Looked out the window. The fog was now rolling in across the far edges of the backyard. Already, the hedges that marked the Laughlins' property had vanished beneath a pillowy whiteness. Already, Tom could see hulking, limping shadows moving in that whiteness. The malevolents. Coming back for him.

He stood up, the chair scraping the floor beneath him. He had to go. He had to find his memory, find the truth. He had to get to the school, to the *Sentinel*'s office.

And that meant he had to leave the house and go out into the fog.

16.

He felt the fear flare inside him as he moved down the hall to the stairs. But he felt something else, too: the old pulse of curiosity, the old fever for the answers. As he passed the front door, he glanced out the sidelight. He glimpsed the thickening sheets of mist covering the front lawn. Pretty frightening—but there was no point in dwelling on it. He turned away and dashed up the stairs, taking two at a time.

Into his bedroom. The baseball bat—the Louisville Slugger Warrior—was back in his closet, as if he'd never removed it. He reached in and felt the cool of the aluminum against his hand. It made him feel a little better to grip the bat and bring it out. He was going to need a weapon out there. The Warrior wasn't much, but it was all he had.

He went to the computer table. Collected his phone and his keys. He started back to the bedroom door—and as he did, there was a soft sound behind him. A brief electronic sizzle, almost like a whisper. Tom stopped in his tracks. He knew where the sound was coming from. The computer. He glanced over his shoulder at it. The little whisper of sound came again, and at the same time there was the faintest hint of light in the depths of the monitor, the faintest appearance of a shape, a silhouetted figure.

Something was in there. Someone. Trying to get out. Trying to talk to him.

The Lying Man.

Tom stood where he was a moment. He was tempted to wait, tempted to listen. It was just that this place—his house, his empty house—was so lonely now. And he was afraid, afraid of going outside. The musical, soothing sound of the Lying Man's voice would be some sort of company, some sort of comfort, even if it told him lies.

It cost Tom a measure of will to turn away, but he did

turn away. Lies were of no use to him now. Before the computer could make another noise, he hurried out the door, carrying his baseball bat with him.

Back down the hall. Back down the stairs. Back to the front door. He pulled it open.

A heaviness came into his belly; a darkness came into his heart. The forward wall of the marine layer had now crept up over the edge of the driveway and was tumbling steadily toward him. He couldn't see the malevolents in the depths of the whiteness yet, but he knew they were there. Close. Getting closer.

Here we go, he thought.

He stepped out of the house and pulled the door shut behind him.

His heart beat hard, and the fear coursed through him like blood as he headed up the driveway to the garage door. His mind was crowded with a thousand doubts and reconsiderations. What if Lisa was wrong? What if he should have stayed in the house and toughed it out? What if Marie was right and he needed to get to the monastery as quickly as he could? He wished Burt was around to help him figure out whom to trust, whom to believe.

He reached the garage door. Took a nervous glance over his shoulder to make sure none of the creatures were sneaking up on him. The main body of the fogbank was still down toward the end of the drive, though the mist up on the lawn was denser than it had been even a few minutes ago.

Taking a deep breath, he turned his back on the scene. He stooped down and grabbed the garage door handle and rolled the door upward.

Burt's old yellow Mustang sat inside in the shadows. Tom moved to the driver's door, unlocked it, and slipped in behind the wheel.

He moved fast, trying to outrun his doubts. He shut the door. Stowed the baseball bat on the passenger side, wedging it half upright between the seat and the door so he could grab it fast if he had to. He snapped on his seat belt. Worked the key into the ignition and switched the engine on. With a deep breath, he shifted to look out through the rear window. He backed out of the garage slowly, backed down the driveway slowly, rolling toward the wall of mist.

The car backed into the street—and the fog closed over it. Wrangling the Mustang's transmission stick into Drive, Tom faced front. The white mass was plastered to the windshield, blotting out the view. He could barely see past the car's hood. He turned on the wipers. They swiped away the condensation on the glass, making it clearer. He turned on the headlights. They carved out about three feet of visibility in front of his fenders. That was as good as it was going to get. He was going to have to take this slow.

He pressed the gas pedal down gingerly. The car started rolling forward at about fifteen miles an hour. Any faster than that and he'd be barreling blind through the fog. And yet every instinct he had urged him to go faster, to get through this mess, to get to the school, to get back indoors as quickly as possible. It took all his restraint to keep the Mustang's speed under control.

Slowly—so slowly—he rolled down the street. His breath came shallow. His heart beat hard. He cast his eyes briefly to the right and left as he moved, peering through the fog to see what he could. Mostly: nothing. White on cloudy white. But now and then he thought he caught a hint, a shadow, a shape of—something. Was that the hovering outline of an oak tree? Was that the looming mass of the Willoughby house hunkering right by the curb at the corner? Yes. The mist shifted a little and he got a clearer look at the old place. All the windows in the house were dark. No one home. No one home anywhere. Tom knew he was all alone out here.

He looked ahead, out the windshield—and let out a gasp as a hulking figure appeared at the edge of his headlights' glow. It vanished almost immediately back into the mist. Gone.

Tom took a few hard breaths, trying to steady himself. He could feel his palms sweating on the steering wheel. The Mustang rolled on—slowly, slowly. He reached the end of his street, where it met with Eucalyptus Road. That was the broad, straight, open avenue that led north to Highway 182, where the school was. The stop sign became visible just before he reached the intersection, but Tom was afraid to halt the car. He was afraid the malevolents would seize the opportunity, that they would come swarming out of the fog and surround him, block his car, break in and devour him. He knew they were out there, just waiting for their chance.

He went right past the stop sign without even slowing. *Hey, let the police pull me over*, he thought. Really, there was nothing in this world he would have liked better than to see a cop right now, traffic ticket and all!

He turned the Mustang onto Eucalyptus. On the wider street, the fog seemed to spread out and become a bit thinner. He lifted his eyes from the small patch of road directly in front of him and scanned the scene through the windshield. He could make out houses like shadows, and the low broad shape of the YMCA building, and the modest spire of the Hope Church where he and his mom went, and where Burt used to go, too. His eyes lingered for a moment on the church as he remembered those mornings when they had all sat together . . .

But then, something—a movement in the mist—caught his attention. He turned toward it.

There they were. Two—no, three—no, wait, four—limping shadows, hulking in the mist: one on a lawn, one in a driveway, one outside the Y, one by the curb. One, that last one, was close enough so that Tom could make him out clearly through the drifting marine layer. He could make out that bizarre and awful elongated face. He could see those red and hungry eyes. They watched him drive past. Once again, he had to fight the urge to hit the gas, to try to race away.

Keep it slow. Keep it steady. They can't touch you if you're in the car, if you're on the move. If you make a run for it in this fog, you'll crash, he told himself, *and then they'll have you.*

He forced himself to focus forward, and he drove on.

The malevolents slipped away behind him. Now there was nothing again, nothing but the fog. Tom's pulse began to slow. His breathing began to even out.

Then the radio started playing.

It was so startling he nearly jumped out of his seat. All at once, the digital display lit up and the car filled with the sound of static. The next moment the numbers on the display started to change, climb. The radio was scanning, looking for a channel. As the numbers on the readout shifted rapidly, the whisper of white noise wavered and dimmed. For a second, Tom heard a snippet of music, a note or two. Then it was gone. The next second he heard a weatherman's voice: "No break in the dense . . ." Then that, too, disappeared into the static as the readout numbers continued to roll on.

The next sound, though . . . the next sound distressed him. Just for a moment, dimly under the white whisper, Tom heard a woman weeping, sobbing.

Was that his mom? Was that his mom crying for him?

Before he could be sure, the noise was gone. There was another snippet of music under the hiss of static. It sounded like a rock band performing in the belly of a giant snake. Then that music, too, dissolved.

Enough, Tom thought.

He reached out to the Off button and pushed it. It had no effect. The radio kept scanning. The static went on. Holding the steering wheel with one hand, Tom tried to hit the button again.

And a voice spoke to him out of the radio with shocking clarity, "Don't touch that dial, Tom."

He knew at once it was the Lying Man. He recognized the calm, lilting, hypnotic voice. He hit the Off button again—harder—and then again. No change. The readout stayed lit.

The Lying Man said, "No, no, no, Tom. That's no use. I'm with you. Whatever you do. I'm always with you."

Tom had to watch the windshield to keep from running

off the road. He took his hand away from the radio, put it back on the steering wheel.

"Did you think I would abandon you?" the mellow voice continued. "I would never do that. I'm here for you, Tom, even when you try to escape me. I'm not only traveling with you—I'm waiting for you wherever you go. Where are you headed now? To your school? I'll be right there when you arrive. Me and all my friends. You can't get away from us. Ever."

There was a flash of movement at the corner of Tom's eyes. He turned to the side window just in time to see another malevolent limp off into the mist. He tried to swallow, but his throat had gone dry. His neck and back and sides, on the other hand, were pouring clammy sweat.

"It's just like Lisa told you," said the Lying Man. "You're not alone."

"What do you want?" Tom said hoarsely. The Mustang continued its slow passage through the deep mist.

"Oh, it's not about what I want," said the Lying Man with a sound of gentle sympathy and concern. "It's about what you want, Tom. That's what I'm here for. For you. It's all about you."

"I just want to find out the truth," Tom said tersely.

"Well, then that's what I want, too," said the serene voice from the radio. "I want you to find out the truth also. The truth about yourself. About what you're really like. About what your life is really like. And about what you really want more than anything."

The sweat poured off Tom even harder. He shivered with the clammy cold of it. His shirt clung to his skin.

"I don't know what you're talking about," he said.

"I think you do," said the Lying Man. "I think you know deep down. I just think you need a little help to figure it out. I think you need *my* help before you can *really* face the truth."

Tom glanced at the radio. He sneered. "I know you," he said, his voice trembling. "I know what you're like now. You lied to me. You're nothing but lies. You're . . ."

At that moment, with a horrible *thud*, something—someone—smashed into his fender.

Without thinking, Tom hit the brakes. The tires squealed as the Mustang skidded to a stop. Tom shouted in fear as a figure tumbled out of the fog and collapsed over the side of the Mustang's hood. At first, he thought it must be a malevolent. But it wasn't. It was a man.

Sprawled over the front of the car, the man looked up through the windshield, looked at Tom desperately. His forehead was streaked with blood. His eyes were wide and shining with a sick brightness. His expression was one of terror.

Shocked, Tom realized he knew the man. He recognized

him. It was the lanky, long-haired young guy from the heavenly garden. The man with the sunken cheeks and hollow eyes, the addict he'd seen on television lying in the hospital bed next to his.

Slowly, the man raised one hand, his wrist bandaged. He reached out desperately as if trying to touch Tom's face through the windshield glass.

Then, in the very next second, before Tom could react, two of the hungry-eyed malevolents lunged out of the surrounding whiteness and seized the man in their poisonous hands. The man shrieked in terror as the creatures' long claws dug into the flesh of his arms. He shrieked again as, gibbering, the malevolents dragged him off the car's hood. The man went on screaming and screaming, but it was no use. With wild cries of triumph, the creatures hauled him away into the mist.

The calm voice on the radio gave a warm laugh. "Now there's a man who finally got what *he* wanted," he said.

Openmouthed, Tom stared out the windshield at the place where the long-haired man had been. The whole awful scene had happened in an instant, and another instant passed before Tom could break through his horror and amazement and act. Then, quickly, he reached for the baseball bat next to the seat beside him. He had to do something. He had to . . . what? He didn't know. Would he go out there?

Try to fight the monsters? Try to save the man? What chance did he have?

It didn't matter. He had to try. He wrapped his fingers around the Warrior and turned back to the windshield, grabbing hold of the door handle with his other hand, ready to leap out.

But it was already too late. The fog swirled and tumbled past the Mustang's windows, deep and thick and empty. The long-haired man had vanished. And what Tom saw next filled his whole body with an acid fear.

The malevolents. They were coming for him. They were everywhere.

17.

His car had been stopped too long. The monsters had spotted him. They were swarming around him now, hunched figures limping and hunkering toward him out of the mist, becoming visible on every side of the Mustang, at every window.

There were two right in front of him, their raw, hideous, misshapen faces caught in the out-glow of his headlights. They were approaching the hood of his car, their arms raised for attack, their clawed fingers reaching. There were more of them to his left, out the driver's window. Three more hungry-eyed beasts slouching out of the drifting whiteness, closing on him. Two more to his right, coming toward the passenger window. And when he looked up into his rearview mirror, he saw the lumbering figures coming up behind him, too.

He was surrounded. There was no way past them.

"I told you, Tom," the Lying Man said quietly over the radio. "You're never alone."

Tom's muscles had gone weak with terror. Second after second as the creatures closed in on him, as they limped closer and closer toward the car from every side, he sat behind the wheel frozen, unable to will himself to move. The monsters in front of him reached his fenders. Their claws were on his car, scraping horribly against the metal. They were beginning to climb up onto the hood, making the Mustang rock. Tom's heart pounded as one of the malevolents reached his door. He heard its claws scraping at the door's handle. And now another one started pounding at the passenger window, trying to break through the glass. And the car rocked even harder as yet another of the things started to climb onto the trunk in back.

"There's nothing to be afraid of, Tom," said the Lying Man. "Soon you and I will be together forever."

Tom let out a roar and hit the gas. The Mustang's tires

squealed and the car shot forward. The monsters on the hood went flying off to either side. For another second—and then another—Tom saw the creatures at the windows running alongside him, hanging on to the doors, trying to keep him from getting away. But the car kept racing forward. The malevolents lost their grip and tumbled off into the mist. Tom kept roaring, kept the gas pedal pressed down hard beneath his sneaker.

The car broke out of the closing circle of creatures and shot away. Tom was free—free but blind because now the mist was thick again, tight against the windows again, and the car was speeding, speeding through a swirling, cottony mass in which he could see nothing.

Moving so blindly at such a speed, Tom quickly lost his sense of direction. He didn't know where the road was. He didn't know where he was going.

There was one more giddy second of racing blindness. Then the Mustang hit the curb, bounced up over the sidewalk, and smashed into a tree.

The car stopped. The engine died. The fog closed in around him.

18.

n that first moment of impact, there was a crunch of
metal, a clatter of shattering plastic, a tinkle of breaking
glass. The left side of the fender collapsed as it smacked
into the tree trunk. The left headlight disintegrated. The jolt
threw Tom forward against the seat belt, and the belt threw
him back against the seat. He was dazed for a moment—but
only for a moment. He willed his mind clear. There was no
time to waste.

The malevolents would catch up to him in seconds. With the car dead, he'd have no chance to escape.

He grabbed the ignition key, wrenched it over, trying to start the car again. The engine wheezed and coughed but wouldn't catch. He could see smoke beginning to pour up from beneath the hood. No, it was no good. The Mustang was finished.

Time to go.

He grabbed the baseball bat. Yanked it out of its space by the door. He glanced through his window to see if the path was clear. He saw the malevolents, dim in the thick fog, but getting clearer every second as they came humping after him.

Moving with the speed of panic, Tom pressed the button to release his seat belt. He grabbed the door handle. Pushed the door open. Dragging the Warrior with him, he tumbled out into the mist.

The cold, damp air closed over him, chilling his cold, damp skin. But it wasn't just the air that chilled him. It was the beasts. So near. He could see their dark shapes. He could hear the brusque grunts of their breathing, the shuffling rhythm of their oncoming footsteps. Without the car around him, he felt totally vulnerable—he *was* totally vulnerable. He had to get out of here. Now.

He'd lost his sense of direction. He wasn't sure where he

was. He wasn't sure which way to go. But the monsters were closing in to the left of him, so he turned to the right, made his way around the fender of the car, and headed into the white murk.

The fog embraced him. Moving blindly, he half ran, half staggered forward. Guessing the direction, he tried to angle his way back to the road. He got it right. A few steps and he stumbled over the curb—nearly tripped, nearly went down, but was then running over the open asphalt with the mist drifting by his face.

He felt afraid. Worse than afraid. He felt hopeless. The fog was everywhere. The creatures were everywhere. He didn't know where he was. He couldn't see where he was going. How could he ever expect to escape?

The voice of the Lying Man played in his head.

I'm waiting for you wherever you go. Where are you headed now? To your school? I'll be right there when you arrive. Me and all my friends. You can't get away from us.

Maybe he was right, Tom thought. Maybe going to the school was a mistake. Or maybe the Lying Man was just trying to scare him, to keep him away from the place where his memory was, where the truth was.

Yes, Tom thought. Yes, that was it. The Lying Man would say anything to keep him from finding out the truth, to keep him from . . .

His thoughts were cut off by a high, hollow, echoing shriek as a malevolent lunged out of the fog, reaching for him.

Tom screamed and twisted away. He felt the thing's claws slice through his sleeve and nick his shoulder. He felt darkness swim up through his mind at the poisonous contact. He staggered back, nauseous, unsteady. The malevolent recovered its balance, turned, preparing to lunge again. Tom braced himself. He grabbed the Warrior bat in both hands. He pulled it back over his shoulders.

With another awful shriek, the malevolent rushed at him again, its distorted features careering toward him out of the fog.

Tom swung with all his might, swung for the fences.

The bat connected—but it wasn't a good hit. The creature was too close. It jammed him. The thinner midsection of the bat struck the beast on the arm. The impact wasn't solid enough to knock it down. But the thing did stagger a few steps to the side. That gave Tom the chance to dance away from it, stepping back quickly out of its reach.

He almost bumped into the malevolent right behind him. Fortunately, the thing let out an eager, hungry shriek and Tom heard it. He spun around—just in time—the beast was nearly on him. It was lurching forward, its eyes gleaming, its dagger-like claws extended toward his face.

There was no time for Tom to bring the bat around

again, so he jabbed with the head of it. It hit the malevolent in the throat. The creature gagged, and a nauseating green slime came out of its mouth as it tumbled over, clutching at its own neck. It fell to the pavement, writhing and choking and spitting.

Tom didn't pause to watch. He knew the first beast was coming after him. He turned—and there it was, nearly on top of him. And here came the others, an army of hulking shadows limping toward him out of the swirling white.

The closest creature gave a high-pitched snarl, its sunken nostrils flaring at the scent of him, its eyes bright with hunger.

Tom heard Lisa's voice as if she were whispering into his ear: *The doctors say if they lose you again, if your heart stops beating again, they doubt they'll be able to revive you. They doubt you'll be strong enough to make it back.*

He didn't hesitate. He cocked the bat again and swung full force. There was a sickening *thud* as he made home-run contact with the nearest creature's head.

What happened next was too disgusting to describe. Even the howl the creature made was so awful that Tom, hearing it, felt as if his blood had turned to ice. In the next second, what was left of the malevolent was writhing at Tom's feet, transforming, smoking, boiling and bubbling into a hideous goo.

Tom took one second to gape at the mess where the creature had been. But that was all the time he had. The rest of them were closing in fast; the one in the lead was so near that Tom could see its burning eyes and the white flash of its sharp teeth.

He turned. He saw the other monster—the one he'd hit in the throat—lying in his path. It was also starting to smoke and melt, its substance bubbling and dissolving into the pavement.

Tom took a long step and leapt over the thing where it lay.

He ran.

19.

He ran—and the mist surrounded him. It chilled him and turned his sweat cold and clammy. The fog was so thick he couldn't see two feet ahead of himself. With each step he expected one of the beasts to loom suddenly out of the whiteness in front of him. Now and then, as he raced on blindly, he caught a glimpse of the things hunched and skulking in the depths of the white. They were keeping pace with him, tracking him, waiting for him to get tired, waiting for him to stop and rest so they could close in for the kill.

And he *was* getting tired. He was already out of breath. His legs were beginning to ache. His lungs were burning. His speed was beginning to dwindle away. He couldn't keep this pace up much longer. He needed to rest.

He dared to take a look back over his shoulder now. Nothing but whiteness. He looked forward. Whiteness. He glanced to the right and the left. White and white. Maybe he'd lost them. Maybe he could pause for just a moment . . .

He slowed to a jog. He slowed to a walk. Almost at once, he heard a bizarre, echoing squeal right behind him. He spun to look, panting.

"Oh no," he whispered.

The fog was suddenly full of them. So many. A whole army, it looked like. Close and moving in. He could hear the harsh snorts of their breathing. He could hear the whisper of their shuffling footsteps. He could see them slumping closer and closer, their forms becoming clearer and clearer as they moved in on him step by slow step.

Just then he heard something new. A soft whisper. A gentle rattling noise above his head.

It was the wind. Now he could feel it. The wind was lifting, stirring the leaves on the trees. The fog began to move and shift with the current of it. Tom began to hope: maybe . . .

He looked around. Yes, there, in the direction he'd been running: the mist was growing thinner.

The wind continued to blow. The mist continued to disperse. Slowly, something new was becoming visible in the whiteness.

What was it? He wasn't sure at first. Just a cluster of strange shapes and shadows. He couldn't figure out what they were. But there was no time to think about it. The malevolents were closing in, dozens of them. Another few seconds and they'd be on him. They'd tear him to pieces. He had to go toward where the fog was parting.

Even with death so near, he had to force his weary legs to move. Ignoring the ache of his muscles, ignoring the burning sensation in his lungs, he started running again.

The wind grew stronger. The fog tumbled dizzyingly around him, leaving him disoriented, off-balance. Still, he managed to stumble toward those bizarre shapes in front of him. They started to become clearer. Now he began to see them through the mist. Was it possible they were . . . ? Yes . . .

Tom felt the hope swell inside him. With his last reserves of energy, he put on an extra burst of speed. The fog continued to thin around him as the wind grew stronger. He ran—and finally, the great mass of mist parted, parted as if a pair of huge hands had seized it on either side and pulled it open like curtains. The edges of white drew apart, threads and tendrils lingering between them. And then even the tendrils blew away and the scene was revealed.

He was in the playground. He had stumbled into the playground of the lower school. It was a sandy pit filled with equipment and structures. Those weird shapes he'd seen— they were the climbing frame, the slide, the crawling tube, the seesaw, and the carousel. Once the fog was peeled away from them, their colorful plastic shapes weren't strange to him at all. He passed this playground on the way to school every day. He knew it well. He'd played here as a little kid.

Quickly, Tom looked around. The wind had blown the fog back from the edges of the sandpit. It was as if an invisible barrier was holding the mist at bay. Tom could still see the monsters in the whiteness behind him. He could still hear them shuffling and grunting. But they couldn't come any closer. They couldn't breach the fog to enter the clearer playground. They drifted back and forth in the mist in hungry frustration.

He was safe. For the moment.

Exhausted, gasping for breath, weak with relief, Tom felt his knees go wobbly under him. The Warrior bat dropped from his trembling fingers, making a metallic sound as it hit the sand. He staggered and had to grab hold of the climbing frame's post to keep himself up. His eyes lifted and he saw— he almost couldn't believe it—he saw the sky! The blue sky made pale by the last thin layer of mist. Could it be that the fog was clearing?

It was. He leaned on the frame and peered off into the distance. The wind continued to stir and the fog continued to blow away from before him.

And now, like a magic city emerging from the clouds, a welcome and familiar scene appeared. A grassy hill. A winding asphalt path along the top of the slope. And at the peak: the school, his school, Springland High.

He was almost there!

Tom would never have thought he could be so glad to see the place. The school was not exactly a crystal fairy-tale palace to look at. Just a sprawling one-story structure of brick, metal, and glass. It was a building Tom came to almost every day. He had become so used to the sight of it that he hardly noticed it at all most of the time. If you had asked him, he would have had to think for a minute before he could say what it looked like. But he noticed it now, all right. He saw it clearly. And what it looked like to him was a refuge, a place to hide, a place to get away from the army of murderous creatures behind him and begin to find the answers he so desperately needed. The woman in the white blouse. The address he'd scribbled down and left in the office of the *Sentinel*. The path back into his memory and the secret of what was keeping him in this coma, so close to death.

He had to get up that hill. He had to hurry, too. He did

not know how long the wind would continue blowing, how long the fog would hold off.

He pushed wearily away from the climbing frame until he was standing on his own. He looked back into the mist out of which he'd come.

The malevolents were still there, still milling along the edges of the marine layer. They snarled and pawed at the churning whiteness as if hoping to break through into the clear. But they couldn't do it.

Tom turned away from them, turned back toward the school. The wind continued to blow, making a path for him through the mist, a clear path up the hill. He took a step toward it.

Remember the Warrior.

Right. He'd nearly forgotten. He bent down and picked the baseball bat up out of the sand. Then, gripping the Warrior in one hand, he started moving. He trudged over the playground sand to the edge of the grass. He started up the hill.

It was slow going. His legs were so tired from running. He was still out of breath. Even this small climb was an effort. His shoulders slumped, the bat bumping over the sod behind him, he trudged upward.

He was just about halfway to the top when there was a new noise. A dark rumble inside the rising rush of the wind. Thunder. Tom felt a fresh twinge of anxiety. The last time it had started to rain, the monsters had gotten him. He couldn't let that happen again.

He paused. The cold air rushed over him. He could feel the storm coming. He looked back down the hill. The pillowy whiteness of the fog was on the move again. It was beginning to roil with the wind. It was starting to roll forward, over the edges of the playground where Tom had just been. Even as he stood there watching, the climbing frame began to fade and grow dim, then the seesaw . . .

The fog was coming after him. And with the fog came the malevolents. Tom could see them moving into the playground, limping amid the equipment, searching for him.

Another low rumble of thunder. No time to waste. He faced forward again, up the hill, toward the school. But before he started moving, he saw something that made him pull up short. Something inside the school. Something alive.

There was a long line of windows in the front of the school. They were tall, the panes starting just off the ground and rising to about shoulder height. The lights were off inside the building and the windows were dark. But as Tom looked, he was almost sure he saw a slow movement behind the unlit glass.

Where are you headed now? To your school? I'll be right there when you arrive.

Tom shuddered at the memory of the Lying Man's promise—or was it a threat? Were the Lying Man and the creatures he controlled already ahead of him? Were they already waiting for him inside the building?

He swallowed. He glanced back over his shoulder. The wind continued to blow and the fog continued rolling toward him up the hill. Already, most of the playground equipment had disappeared in the whiteness. Already, the first of the malevolents were limping toward the bottom of the slope.

Tom had no choice. He had come this far. There was nowhere to go but forward.

He began to climb the hill again. He neared the school slowly. He reached the path at the top of the slope. Just as he did, another movement at one of the school's windows caught his eye.

This time it was unmistakable. A figure was emerging from the darkness inside the school. It was approaching the window.

The thunder rolled. The wind blew. The fog rolled toward him up the hill.

The figure inside the school became clearer—and even more clear. It pressed itself against the glass and looked out at him.

"Gordon?" said Tom out loud—but his voice was lost in a fresh rumble of thunder.

It was. It was Gordon. The Tigers football star stood for a moment, pressed to the window. He peered out at Tom with a strangely empty expression on his face. Slowly, he lifted his hand in greeting.

But before Tom could respond, the thunder rolled again like dark laughter. There was a first flash of lightning. And Gordon drew back into the darkness of the school's interior and vanished like a ghost.

INTERLUDE THREE

There came a nightmare day. A Wednesday afternoon. The last class period but one. For Tom, that meant PE. He and ten other guys doing gymnastics, climbing ropes in the gym, working on the horse and the beams and the mats and so on. When the class was over, the guys headed into the locker room. They showered. They got back into their street clothes. Tom was standing in front of his locker, buttoning his shirt, when he felt that something was wrong.

He looked up. Looked around him. Where was everyone? Somehow, while he was concentrating on getting dressed, all the other guys had quietly slipped out of the locker room. The place was empty. He was alone.

Alone—and then not alone. The locker room door opened

and three guys came in. Not just any three guys. Three Tigers. Big Tigers, too—jumbo size—from the defensive line: Matt Halliwell, Hank Thatcher, and Dub Simpson.

As Tom stood staring, they moved in on him. They stood around him in a semicircle. Tom's back was against his gym locker. There was nowhere for him to run.

Tom's fingers were still fiddling with the last button on his shirt. He didn't even have his sneakers back on yet. He was in his socks. He realized this must've been part of some kind of plan: the other guys slipping out, leaving him alone; the three football players converging on him. His mind raced, trying to think of an escape strategy. He came up with nothing. He felt just about as helpless as it was possible to feel. If these guys wanted to rough him up, he was going to get majorly roughed.

Matt Halliwell spoke first. Broad-shouldered, fat-faced, flat-faced, with black hair so short it looked like iron filings standing up on top of a magnet. He put a finger the size of a sausage against Tom's chest. Poked him hard.

"Nice story you wrote about us, wimp," he said.

Dub Simpson, shaped like a cinder block and about as smart as a cinder block, shoved Tom's shoulder with his open palm.

"What'd you have to do that for?" he said.

Tom's eyes flashed from Matt to Dub—and then to Hank

Thatcher. Hank looked away, frowning. What a weird situation this was! Hank was one of the sources for Tom's story. Hank had been a benchwarmer on the championship team three years before. He had seen the players taking drugs himself. He had pictures of them and e-mails from them proving it. He had met Tom in a parking garage one dark night. Handed the evidence over in a rolled-up manila envelope. But he had given Tom that information on the condition of anonymity. Tom had promised never to reveal his name. And now Hank, to protect his secret from his teammates, was joining with the others in taking vengeance on him— and Tom was bound by his promise to keep his mouth shut about it. If this was irony, then irony stank.

"You should've kept your stupid opinions to yourself," said Matt, poking him in the chest again.

"Nobody asked you what you thought," said Dub.

"It's not what I thought," Tom said. He figured, well, if he was going to get a beat-down, he wasn't going to whine about it. He was going to say his piece at least, while he still had his teeth. "It has nothing to do with my opinions. You think I don't like the team? I love the team. My brother played on the team. I didn't want to write this story. I had to. Because it was true."

Dub somehow wasn't interested in hearing about the responsibilities of the press. "They say they may take our championship away," he complained, sticking out his jaw angrily.

Yeah, because you didn't earn it fairly! Tom thought. But he didn't say that out loud. No sense pushing things too far. What he did say was, "Well, look, man, I'm really sorry, but like I said, I'm a news guy, I have to . . ."

"Sorry?" And this time Matt poked him so hard it made him step back into his locker with a clang. "What good does sorry do us now? You're supposed to be loyal to the school, man! You're supposed to stand with the team."

Tom could see this was about to get ugly. He could see that Matt was working himself up to do violence and that Dub was already on the brink—Dub was pretty much always on the brink. And Hank was not going to do a thing to stop either of them because that would give him away.

But just as Tom was wondering how he was going to explain his broken bones to his mother, the locker room door opened again and in came Gordon Thomas.

———

One of the secret truths of the world, Tom had sometimes noticed, was that life is unfair and that some people get all the luck. This truth was so harsh that many adults couldn't face up to it. But a kid only had to step out onto a playground once to understand: some people are born smarter, some faster, some stronger, some simply cooler than the rest. Parents and teachers worked hard to convince kids that everyone was special, but kids could see for themselves it wasn't so—otherwise, the word *special* wouldn't mean anything. Every soul was important, sure—a unique work of creation—but when it came to the gifts of nature, most people were kind of ordinary. Only special people were special.

Gordon Thomas was one of those special people. He was handsome with chiseled features and reddish-blond hair that fell rakishly into his startlingly pale blue eyes. Fast and strong? Check. No one had ever beaten him in a race. No one ever tried to beat him in a fight. He was even smart—maybe not as smart as some of the geeks in school, but he always paid attention in class, always did his homework, and always got good grades. And as for being cool, it just came naturally to him. For all his gifts, he wasn't arrogant or stuck-up. For all his physical strength, he never bullied anyone. For all his success, he always acted modestly and treated people decently. So you couldn't even hate the guy!

And Tom didn't hate him. He envied him sometimes. But he liked him. Everyone liked him.

Gordon came into the locker room fast now, and he

looked angry. Quickly, he shoved his way past Matt and muscled in between him and Tom, shielding Tom from the others with his body.

"What d'you guys think you're doing?" Gordon asked them. He looked at each in turn: Matt, Hank, Dub. All three of them averted their eyes, shamefaced in front of the quarterback. "What, are the Tigers beating guys up now? Are we thugs all of a sudden?"

"We're just talking to him," Matt muttered.

"Oh yeah," said Gordon. "I can see."

The three linemen looked at their shoes, ashamed.

"Coach says they may take our trophy away," said Dub. "It's not fair."

"It's not fair?" said Gordon, staring hard at the cinder block. "How is it not fair? It wasn't fair when our guys took drugs to win. That wasn't fair to the Sandy Hill Panthers, who should've gotten the trophy in the first place. All Tom did was tell the truth about it. How is that not fair?"

Dub blinked stupidly. Dub did that a lot. "He wasn't loyal to the team," he grumbled.

"Well, maybe he was loyal to something bigger than the team," said Gordon—though even he sounded miserable about it. "It's his job to tell the truth even when he doesn't like it. Maybe especially when he doesn't like it. He was loyal to that."

"We just wanted to make him understand what he did to us," said Matt.

"I know what you just wanted to do," Gordon said. "But the facts don't go away just because you beat up the guy who tells them. That just makes you as bad as the guys who took the dope. You want the trophy back?"

"Yeah!" said Dub.

"Well, then let's win it back," Gordon said quietly. "If we do it right, we don't have to be afraid of what anyone says."

Dub blinked stupidly some more, but even he seemed to grasp this concept. Sort of.

"Now get out of here," said the quarterback. "Leave Tom alone. He didn't do anything wrong. And anyone who messes with him, messes with me."

That was Gordon—typical Gordon. And that was why, when all the players had gone, when Gordon was gone and Tom was alone in the locker room again, he sank down slowly onto one of the benches.

Because he felt bad—really bad. It was true he hadn't written the story about the team because he hated the team or because he was envious of Gordon, and he hadn't done it to impress Marie. He had written the story because it was the truth and telling the truth was something he did, something he felt the need to do. But whatever his motives had been, the results had been the same: he'd gotten the team in trouble and hurt Gordon and won Marie's admiration. It made Tom feel guilty, as if those had been his motives after all.

———

He especially felt guilty when he was hanging out with Marie. And he was hanging out with her more and more now. The very next weekend, the next Sunday afternoon, he was at her house after church. He joined her and her father and mother and brother for lunch.

The Cameron mansion was even more impressive inside than outside. When Tom stepped through the front door, he came into a vast foyer with marble floors and a sweeping staircase rising to a second-floor balcony. In the study, where he sat with Marie before lunch was served, there were photographs everywhere. Dr. Cameron shaking hands with the mayor. Dr. Cameron with his arm around the governor's shoulder. Dr. Cameron laughing with the owner of the Dodgers. Dr. Cameron with just about every famous person who lived anywhere near town.

When it was time to eat, they all sat in a vast dining room with a wall of glass doors that looked out across the hillside at the sparkling Pacific Ocean. Dr. Cameron sat at one end of the long glass table and Mrs. Cameron at the other.

Marie's brother, Carl, was on one side, and Marie and Tom sat next to each other across from him. The room was bright with sunlight. The light hit the prisms in the chandelier and was turned into rainbows and the rainbows fell on the crystal goblets and the china plates and the hand-carved oak sideboard against the wall. Tom felt as if he had stepped into a world so plush and beautiful as to have an aura of magic.

Dr. Cameron lifted a glass of orange juice in a toast to him. He was a tall, trim, broad-shouldered man with a face as perfect as his daughter's, his hair a silvery blond. "Marie has told us so much about you, Tom," he said with a smile. He had a calm, reassuring voice—a good voice for a doctor, Tom thought. "We're really glad to know we'll be seeing more of you around here in the future."

Tom was glad to know this, too—it was the first he'd heard of it! But Marie seemed to agree. She smiled in that way that made Tom ache.

It was a wonderful lunch. Tom talked about his work at the newspaper. He talked about his story, the one about the football team, and how he was working on new leads. Instead of being angry at him, Marie and her family admired him. It was a nice change from being at school.

After lunch, Marie walked him over the broad front lawn of her house to where Tom's Mustang was parked at the curb.

"Daddy really likes you," she said. She took hold of his arm as they reached the car. She pressed close to him. "That's a really good thing, you know. He's the best guy in the world. And he knows a lot of important people—all the important people around here, for sure! He can be a really good friend to you, Tom, when you're applying to colleges or looking for a job, all that stuff."

"Yeah, well, he seems like a really good guy," Tom said. And he thought he could probably use some help applying to colleges now that the principal and all his teachers hated him.

They reached his car. Tom turned to look at her. He wanted to ask her about Gordon then. He wanted to make sure everything was over between them, that there would be no hard feelings about him moving in on Gordon's girl or anything like that. But he didn't say a word. With Marie holding his arm and looking up at him the way she was, he didn't want to do anything that might ruin the moment.

He was still trying to convince himself to speak when Marie suddenly moved in even closer and kissed him.

At which point Tom completely forgot about Gordon Thomas, and about everything.

20.

Urged on by the wind and thunder, Tom hurried over the last yards of the hill to the school's front door. The door was made of glass and was dark, like the windows. As he approached it, he thought he saw another figure within, but it was only his own reflection. It was the first time he'd seen himself since he left the house. He was shocked by his expression of wild-eyed panic. With the baseball bat gripped in his fist, he looked like some sort of madman ready to bust up the world.

The wind blew harder, with a hollow roar like the sea's. It carried the first drops of rain in it. Tom felt them on his neck and cheeks. He tried the door. It was locked. He rattled it, but it wouldn't budge. There was a fresh grumble of thunder. It sounded—weirdly—like the low laughter of the Lying Man. Tom looked over his shoulder, half expecting to see the man himself standing right there behind him. What he saw was almost as scary: the first tendrils of mist were swirling up the hill after him. The fog—and the malevolents within it—were on their way.

He rattled the school door again.

"Gordon?" he shouted. "Are you in there? Let me in! I need to get in!"

There was no answer.

"Gordon!"

An electric crackle made Tom stiffen. White light flashed around him, making his image on the glass door transparent and phantom-like. Lightning. The storm was beginning again. He didn't want to be exposed out here when it struck. He had to get inside fast.

He stepped back from the door. He lifted the Louisville Slugger in his two hands.

Well, he thought, *since I'm inside my own mind, I guess this isn't a crime.*

He jabbed the head of the bat at the glass door. Then

he did it again. That second time did the trick. With a loud crack, a triangle of glass broke away from the rest of the pane. The shard fell into the school and Tom heard it shatter on the floor in there. He reached through the hole, hoping to find a latch, but the door had a key lock. There was no way to undo it. So, as the thunder rolled again—the thunder that sounded like eerie laughter—Tom worked quickly, jabbing through the glass of the door with his bat head again and again, breaking off piece after piece, clearing a larger and larger hole for himself.

The thunder subsided then, but the wind rose. Tom took one last look behind him. The mist was creeping up the hill, advancing quickly with a slithering motion back and forth across the grass. The air was now laced with thin rain. Tom turned and, stooping low to keep from getting cut, stepped through the hole he'd made in the door and entered the school.

At first there was the noise of glass crunching under his sneakers. But as he moved away from the litter on the floor, the noise stopped and a deep quiet surrounded him, broken only by the steady sough of the wind through the broken door. He was in the school's front lobby, a place he saw almost every day. A broad, open hall decorated with bulletin boards and posters and signs. "Spring Comes to Springland" read a banner in one display case. There were various poems and works of art taped up inside. There were posters for school shows nearby and sign-up sheets for clubs and programs. And there was a trophy case displaying plaques and prizes the school had won: top test scores in the county, winner of a state essay contest—and, of course, the trophy for the state football championship, the one now under investigation because of Tom's story.

Two corridors ran off from the lobby, one on either side of him. The halls were dark, sunk in shadow. Peering into the gloom, he could make out rows of lockers on the corridor walls, their bright green paint muted in the dim light. At first glance, the halls looked empty. But as Tom paused there for a moment, peering down the corridor to his right, he suddenly saw something. He caught his breath. There had been a swift movement in the shadowy reaches at the end. Someone crossing the hall from one side to the other. A moment later Tom heard a door swing shut down there.

"Gordon?" he called.

But there was no answer. No sound at all except the wind through the broken door. The wind that sounded like a whisper.

And then there *was* a whisper: "Tom."

Startled, Tom wheeled around. That sounded like Lisa. Yes! There she was. Or at least he thought he could make her out standing in the shadows down the other hall, down by the principal's office. Just standing there, watching him.

"Lisa?" he said softly, his throat dry. This place was really beginning to spook him.

The figure didn't move, didn't answer. Just stood there, watching him. Creepy. Very.

He started walking toward her slowly. "Lisa?" he said again—though he could barely get the word out now. "Is that you?"

Still, the figure stood motionless. As Tom got closer, the shadows seemed to gather around her. Her shape seemed to blend in with their darkness. As he came even closer, he saw that the darkness was all there was. Lisa had faded away like a mirage, vanishing so smoothly into the shadows that Tom couldn't be sure she had ever been there at all.

He reached the spot where Lisa had been—or where he thought she'd been—about halfway down the hall. It gave him a very eerie feeling to find the place empty.

He was right outside the principal's office now. There was a large pane of glass here. Usually, on a school day, you could look right through the glass and see the outer office where the principal's two assistants worked. But today the glass was completely—weirdly—black. Nothing was visible through it. Nothing at all.

Just then, from behind him—through the glass door he himself had broken—there came a rattling crash of thunder. Lightning flashed almost simultaneously. The electric glow flickered over Tom where he stood—and in that momentary light, Tom caught a glimpse of someone standing on the other side of the principal's window, looking out at him.

Tom gasped—and then his breath came out of him unsteadily. He recognized that half-seen face. It was the Lying Man.

I'm not only traveling with you—I'm waiting for you wherever you go.

"Tom! This way! Hurry!"

With another start, Tom turned toward the whisper. It sounded like Lisa again. And again, there she was—or the ghost of her—standing still and dim in the hall's far shadows.

He took another glance at the principal's window, but it was black again. If the Lying Man was in there, Tom couldn't see him. All the same, he was glad to get away from that place. He moved down the hall toward the figure of Lisa, calling out to her as he went.

"Lisa, is that you? Wait for me."

But she didn't answer him. She stood eerily silent. And eerily, she did the mirage thing again, fading away into the shadows before he could reach her.

Tom's heart was rabbiting inside him. He felt like he was in a haunted house. A school full of phantoms. It was almost more frightening than the fog full of monsters. And the thunder and lightning outside didn't help any either.

"Tommeeee."

Lisa's ghostly whisper drifted to him again, but this time when he looked into the dark, he couldn't see her.

"Tommmeeeeee."

He moved toward the sound. He reached the end of the hallway. There were stairs there, a broad flight going down into the basement.

"Tommmeee."

That's where her voice was coming from.

Was she trying to get him to come down to the *Sentinel*'s office? To get the address he'd left there, the address of the woman in the white blouse? But why haunt him like this? That's where he was headed anyway.

"Tommy, come down," she whispered from the darkness below.

This was just plain creepy now. It reminded him of the time he'd met Hank in the parking garage. He didn't know what he was walking into.

"Come down, Tommy."

He had to do it. He had to get that address. He had to find the woman in the white blouse. He had to remember what he had forgotten—who shot him and why—if he was ever going to get out of his coma. If he was ever going to learn the truth. If he was ever going to make it home alive.

Tom heard the low thunder outside—or was it just the

Lying Man's laughter? He knew there was no going back—not for him, not with the need to know that beat inside him like his own pulse. He had to move.

He started down the stairs. Every nerve in him seemed to be standing on edge. He was listening for any noise, any threat. He reached the bottom and stepped down into yet another dark corridor. He paused, staring into the deep shadows, waiting for his eyes to adjust.

"Tommeee."

He held his breath. Lisa's whisper. And wait . . . someone else now.

". . . just for a little while . . ."

Who was that? He wasn't sure.

"I don't like it . . ." Yet a third voice, a third whisper.

And then more:

"This way, Tom."

"Go to the monastery."

"Why did you do it?"

". . . ruin everything . . ."

Tom finally breathed out, quivering. The corridor was full of whispers, full of ghostly voices.

"He's not your friend."

"The monastery."

"This way, Tommy."

As Tom stared, he thought he saw movements in the

shadows, but the fleeting figures were so faint he wasn't sure they were really there.

Clutching his baseball bat in one hand, he started to edge forward—moving with slow care, barely lifting his feet as he shuffled along.

"Go to the monastery."

"I don't like it."

"It's just for a little while."

"This way."

Tom moved deeper down the hall, deeper into the darkness. He felt a breath of air on his face as something rushed past him. But when he turned to look—nothing—there was nothing there. Only the whispers.

"Tommmeee."

"He's not your friend . . ."

There was another movement. And another. Each time, when Tom looked, there was no one, nothing. And yet the whispers went on as he shuffled slowly forward. It was so bizarre that words finally burst out of him: "Is anyone there? Is anyone . . . ?"

For a moment after he spoke, there was silence. Then— something new. A snap and crackle. A flicker of light. Not lightning—not down here. Instead, it was the wavering purple glow of a fluorescent bulb trying to come on but not quite making it. It was coming through a doorway just ahead to his right, lighting the rectangle of the entrance. Tom knew what room it was. The *Sentinel*'s office. The light flickered again. He moved toward it.

The whispers around him seemed to dim. The movements grew more distant. He reached the open doorway where the light was flickering and stepped through. He reached for the wall. Found the light switch. Pushed it. To his enormous relief, the fluorescents in the ceiling flickered on and stayed on.

The *Sentinel*'s office was empty.

Tom let out a sigh. It was comforting to be back in the familiar place, the cramped little cubicle of a room with the desks jammed into it and papers littering the desktops and the walls. He had spent a lot of happy hours here, sitting with Lisa, working with Lisa, talking over stories with her and just, really, gossiping about stuff. They were some of the best times he'd ever had.

He wove quickly between the desks. Went to the front of his own desk. He leaned the Warrior bat against it. Started pawing through the papers scattered around the base of his computer, searching for a page with the address on it. There were Post-its, notebooks, notices, printouts of articles he'd been writing. Paper clips. Pens. A dead-tree phone book. A syllabus, ditto. But no address. Where was it? Tom began to feel hollow inside. Was it possible he had figured this all wrong? Was it possible he had left his house and braved the fog and the malevolents for nothing? He pawed through the papers more quickly, more frantically. No address.

He stopped. He straightened. He tried to think. The haunted school was silent all around him.

Then, suddenly, that silence was shattered. The phone rang—not the cell in his pocket, but the phone on the desk. The noise was so loud and unexpected he nearly jumped out of his own skin.

He picked up the handset. Spoke uncertainly, "Hello?"

A voice came over the line—also uncertain: "Is this . . . is this the *Sentinel*?"

It was her! It was the woman in the white blouse. The same voice that had tried to speak to him before through the alien static. There was no static now. The voice was clear as a bell.

"Uh . . . yeah. Yeah, this is the *Sentinel*," said Tom.

"I want to speak with Tom Harding."

"This is Tom," he said.

"I need to talk to you. It's very important," said the woman. Her voice was low, as if she was afraid of being overheard.

"All right," said Tom, "I'm listening. Go ahead."

As he spoke the words, Tom had a powerful sense of déjà vu, a powerful sense that he had had this conversation before, lived through this moment before. He felt as if everything that was going to be said now had already *been* said. More than that. He had the strangest feeling that the script of the conversation had already been written, and that he could not speak any other words but the words that he *would* speak.

She's about to tell me that she can't talk over the phone, he thought. *That it's too dangerous.*

"Not now," said the woman. "I can't talk over the phone. It's too dangerous. You have to come to my place. Tomorrow. In person. Alone. I have information you're going to want to hear."

"What kind of information?" said Tom—the words just came out of him. He knew he couldn't say anything else. The script was already written.

"Never mind that now. Just come to my apartment tomorrow at four. My name is Karen Lee. I live at 47 Pinewood Lane. The Pinewood Apartments, apartment 6B. Come alone, and don't tell anyone. Don't let anyone see you."

Without thinking, Tom picked up a pen and scribbled the address down on a Post-it note: *Karen Lee. 47 Pinewood Lane, Apt. 6B.*

"Miss Lee, can you just give me some sort of idea what we'll be talking—" he heard himself begin to say.

But then—as he knew it would—a dial tone interrupted him. The woman had hung up.

Slowly, Tom lowered the handset back into its cradle.

How weird was that? Knowing what she was going to say before she said it. Being unable to answer her in any way but the way he had.

Because it was a memory, Tom realized. *That's why. Because the conversation already happened in the past and I was just remembering.*

He stared at the Post-it note, at the name and address scribbled there. Then he raised his eyes to the door, and to the darkened hallway beyond.

They're all memories! he realized. *Those ghosts out in the hall. Those whispering voices. They're all memories.*

That's why the school was haunted. It was his memory. It was haunted by things that had happened but that he had forgotten since being shot, since lapsing into a coma. He had come here to find a source of information and he had. The source of information was his own mind.

Well then, he had reached his destination, hadn't he? That was the good news. He had found his way into his memory. Now all he had to do was find the trail of memories that would lead him to the truth—the truth about who had shot him, and the reason he couldn't wake up.

Just as he thought that, the lights in the ceiling started to flicker. The *Sentinel's* office went in and out of shadow.

Tom quickly stuffed the Post-it note into his pocket. He picked up the Warrior bat.

The light snapped off. The room was plunged into darkness.

"Tommy."

A whisper from the doorway. He looked. Very faintly, he could make out Lisa's figure.

She beckoned to him.

She whispered: "This way."

21.

By the time he reached the office doorway, Lisa had melted away again into the shadows. He was hardly even surprised this time. But he wondered: why had she been there at all? He had gotten the address he'd come for. Wasn't that what she was trying to lead him to? What else was there?

Tom stepped hesitantly into the hall. Immediately his eye was drawn by a light to his right—a thin line of light running across the floor at the corridor's end. He knew it was coming from underneath the gym's big double doors. Someone was in the gym.

And Lisa—her silhouette—was standing in the nearby shadows.

"This way, Tommy."

There was more she wanted him to see. More he had to remember.

Tom began moving toward the line of light. As he did, he became aware that a new tension had come into his body, a new acid sourness was roiling his stomach. He did not want to do this. He did not want to go to the gym. There was something in there. A memory. A memory he did not want to recover.

That was the trouble with searching for the truth. It wasn't always pleasant. It wasn't always something you wanted to find.

Tom moved reluctantly toward the light beneath the gym doors. He watched Lisa's silhouette meld with the shadows and vanish as he approached. All around him, he heard faint whispers, felt movements as if people were passing by him. Phantoms of things that had happened, things half recalled. He ignored them. They were just distractions now. He kept moving toward the gym.

As he neared the door, he heard muffled voices on the

other side. A guy and a girl, talking. He couldn't make out the words. He heard a clank and a bang. He recognized that sound. Someone was lifting weights. Dropping the weights on the mat.

I came here after school to get my keys, he thought.

He was remembering now. The three guys from the football team had surrounded him in the locker room. Gordon had come to his rescue. In the excitement, Tom had forgotten his keychain, left it in his locker when he went back to his final class. He hadn't noticed the keys were gone until later, after school, after he'd gotten ready to leave the *Sentinel* and head home. Then he went to the gym to recover his keys. He had thought the school was empty by now. But it wasn't.

He reached the gym door. The voices continued within. He put his hand out in the darkness until his fingers brushed the metal bar that released the latch. He pushed the bar gently, opened the door just a crack, just enough for him to see through.

He knew what he would see a moment before he saw it. All the same, the sight—the memory—struck him like a punch.

In the bright light beyond the door, he saw Marie and Gordon. They were at the far end of the gym. Gordon was standing near the wall racks where the free weights hung. He was dressed in shorts and a sleeveless undershirt. He was curling a bar with heavy weights on it. Tom could only guess how much: A hundred pounds? More? Gordon's massive biceps bulged and strained as he brought the bar up from his thighs to his chest.

Marie was sitting in the small bleachers there, sitting on the second tier, watching Gordon lift. Her blond hair was tied back, and she was beautiful in a white blouse and jeans, beautiful as always. She sat leaning back, with her elbows propped on the tier behind her. She never took her eyes off the weight-lifting quarterback.

And even from across the room, the look in Marie's eyes was unmistakable. It was a look of powerful admiration, powerful attraction. And something else, something more. It was a look of . . . What was the right word? *Ownership.* Yes. She was looking at Gordon as if he belonged to her, and as if she belonged to him, too.

Tom had come into the gym when he thought it would be empty, and he was seeing now what he had seen then.

Finishing his set of curls, Gordon gave a grunt and dropped the bar to the floor. The weights bounced against the mat, rattling loudly. Marie and Gordon did not notice him there in the doorway.

Marie shook her head in open admiration. "You are a mighty man, Gordon Thomas," she said. She fluttered her eyelashes comically. "You make my girlish heart go pitterpat."

Gordon couldn't help but smile a little at the flattery, but it was a grim smile and he turned away from her.

Marie rolled her eyes. "Oh, come on, sweetheart, don't be like that, all right?"

"I just don't like it," he said.

Marie leaned forward, her elbows on her knees. "Oh, baby, I know, but it's just for a little while."

Gordon put his hands on his hips. He looked down at his sneakers, shaking his head. "Three of the guys almost shredded him today," he said. "He doesn't deserve that. And he doesn't deserve what you're doing to him either."

"Right!" Marie lifted her eyes heavenward again. "You're such an innocent, Gordon, you know that? You think Tom's your friend. You think he wrote that story because he's some kind of heroic reporter dedicated to telling the truth no matter what. Well, he's not your friend, sweetheart. He's never been your friend. He's been jealous of you since we were in elementary school. And he's had a creepy crush on me since forever, too. *That's* why he wrote that stupid story. To get back at you. And to get to me. Well, now he has me. Or he thinks he does, anyway."

Still standing with his hands on his hips, Gordon looked at her. "It's mean," he said. "It's mean and it's dishonest and . . . I don't like it."

"Oh, baby," said Marie with feeling. "I know. I know, I

know, I know. It's because you're so good, you're so sweet. But I have to do it. Trust me, okay? If I can just make him feel he has a chance with me, I know I can keep him from . . . you know. From writing anything else. I know he'll stop. For me. And he's got to stop. He's got to. Otherwise, he could ruin everything. Oh, come on, baby," she said as Gordon turned his back on her. She climbed down off the rafters now. She went to him. She stood behind him. Put a hand gently on his back, between his shoulder blades. "Come on," she said, her voice soft and coaxing. "It's just for a little while. I promise."

Gordon could not resist her—any more than Tom had been able to resist her. Gordon turned. He wrapped his arms around her. She clung to him, pressing her face against his chest. They held each other fast.

Tom stepped back and let the door close. The light beneath it went out. The memory was over.

He stood in the darkness without moving. He stared at the door in front of his nose. He stared at nothing. All of Marie's sweet smiles. All her admiring words. That kiss outside her house. All lies. All make-believe.

He's had a creepy crush on me since forever.

No wonder he hadn't wanted to remember this. No wonder he'd blanked it out. He could not believe how much it hurt. Next to Burt's death, it hurt more than anything he had ever felt in his life. He understood now why people said they were brokenhearted. It felt that way. He felt as if Marie had tossed his heart to the ground and broken it into a million pieces.

"But why?" he whispered into the dark. Why had she done it? Even in his sorrow, the curiosity that always pulsed at the core of him would not leave him alone.

I know I can keep him from writing anything else. I know he'll stop. For me.

What had she wanted to keep him from writing? The story about the team was already published. Why had she pretended to like him? Why had she hurt him so badly?

"Why?" he whispered again.

In answer, there came a low, casual laugh from behind him.

Tom spun around, clutching the Warrior bat in his two hands.

There in the darkness stood the Lying Man.

22.

The anger went off in Tom like an explosion, a red rage that blasted out of his core and spread all through him.

He had just seen Marie—remembered Marie—revealing her disdain for him, dashing his heart to the ground. And now here was the laughing, conniving, insinuating, threatening, and terrifying Lying Man. And Tom had had enough.

He cocked the bat over his shoulder. He wanted to pound the Lying Man's laughter back into his throat.

But where was he? A moment ago his shadowy presence had been standing right in front of him. That lean, dark face with its smart, bright eyes—that face that somehow sent a chill up his spine—had been smiling at him from no more than a few feet away. And now . . .

Now the laughter came again from a distance. And Tom saw the Lying Man—the shadow of the Lying Man—halfway down the hall.

Furious, he cocked the bat even farther over his shoulder and stepped forward.

"What do you want?" he shouted. "Come on, you coward! What do you want? Stop trying to mess with my mind! Stop playing head games with me! Just come on and say it! What do you want?"

Tom advanced another step, but the Lying Man didn't back away. He didn't seem afraid at all. He stood in a relaxed posture, his eyes glinting in the darkness. Just as before, something about him, something about his half-seen features, sent an icy shiver up Tom's spine. Angry as he was, he felt it. For all the Lying Man's easy laughter, for all the soothing calm of his voice, there was just something terrifying about this guy.

The Lying Man's laughter trailed off into a low chuckle. "I told you, Tom," he said in a tone full of friendship and sympathy. "I only want for you what you want for yourself.

I mean, you wanted the truth, right? Well, now you have it. Now you see. The truth is that Marie doesn't really like you very much at all. All that love you felt for her? All that tenderness and yearning all these years. Marie just thought it was—what was her word?—*creepy*. When she pretended to like and admire you, she was playing with you, my friend. She was playing with you so she could control you, like a puppet on a string—convince you to do whatever she wanted."

Tom came another step closer, brandishing the bat, breathing hard. But he could feel the anger—and the strength—draining out of him. The Lying Man wasn't lying now, was he? He wasn't lying about Marie. That was the truth about her, all right. And just hearing it spoken out loud filled Tom with sorrow—a heartbroken grief that sapped his energy.

The Lying Man seemed to sense this. Rather than retreating from him in fear, he took a casual step toward him. Tom could now see his smile, his teeth gleaming gray in the shadows. For some reason he couldn't name, the sight made his gorge rise into his throat, made him feel he might be sick.

"I know it's painful for you, Tom," said the Lying Man sympathetically. "But better to find out now, right? Better to find out before you make a fool of yourself. Or, that is, before you make a *bigger* fool of yourself than you already have. You see? I've *helped* you, Tom. I've helped you find the truth you were looking for. And here you threaten me with that bat of yours. Where's the sense in that? Why should you be angry at me?"

Tom had no answer. The tide of his sorrow rose within him and the tide of his strength and anger continued to recede. He stopped advancing on the Lying Man. The bat drooped and settled onto his shoulder.

The Lying Man seized the moment and took another easy step toward him. The lean face and its arch features became clearer in the dark—and though Tom felt even more nauseated, somehow he couldn't look away.

"You know what this reminds me of?" the Lying Man said. "Do you remember, Tom, when you wrote that story about the football team? Do you remember how everyone got angry at you? And why? All you'd done was tell the truth. You told the truth and they didn't want to hear it, so instead of facing it squarely, they got angry at you. They got angry at the messenger because they didn't want to hear the message. Isn't that exactly what you're doing to me now? I've shown you a truth you didn't want to know, and now instead of confronting it bravely like a man, you're yelling at me and threatening me! It's a kind of cowardice really, isn't it?" He laughed again, clearly unafraid.

Tom let the bat drop off his shoulders. He let the head

of it sink to the floor. What was he going to do? Brain the guy with it? For what? Talking? Telling the truth about Marie? No. The Lying Man was right. That was just cowardice. There was no point taking his anger out on him. That wouldn't change a thing.

He let a long stream of breath come sighing out of him. He just felt tired now. Exhausted, in fact. Totally played out.

Marie, he thought miserably.

"Oh, don't be too hard on her, Tom," said the Lying Man. It was as if he could hear Tom thinking! "After all, you're not so pure of heart either, are you?"

Tom stood powerless as he watched the Lying Man come another step closer, as the Lying Man moved smoothly into a patch of deeper shadow that nearly obscured him from Tom's view.

"That's part of the truth, too, isn't it?" he said in his serene and reasonable voice. "What Marie said about you. About your motives for writing that story. She has a point, doesn't she? You *were* upset you couldn't be on the team. And you *were* jealous of Gordon, weren't you?"

Tom lowered his chin, looked at the floor. "Sometimes," he muttered. He wished it wasn't so, but it was.

"And you did want to steal Marie away from him."

Tom shook his head weakly. That wasn't why he wrote the story. It was never his reason.

"Are you sure?" said the Lying Man, as if Tom had spoken these words aloud. "Are you absolutely sure those weren't your motives? Are you sure you're not just as much a liar as Marie is? I mean, look at yourself, Tom. Really look at yourself for a change. Look at your life. You've lost your brother. You've lost your friends. You've spent years pining for a girl who despises you. And as for who you are . . . well, you like to think of yourself as a courageous seeker after truth, I know. But I sort of suspect you're just an envious little person trying to use your newspaper to take vengeance on people who are more successful than you are."

Tom stood slumped, unable to find the energy even to answer. Was it true? Was that really his life? Was that really himself? Right then, right after seeing Marie, right after hearing what she said about him and feeling his heart break inside him, he certainly felt . . . well, he felt as miserable as the Lying Man's description of him. He felt worthless. Weak. As if life weren't even worth living.

So maybe the Lying Man wasn't such a liar after all.

Tom slowly lifted his head. He looked down the hall, peered into the shadows in the direction of the Lying Man's voice. But he couldn't see him anymore. The Lying Man seemed to have vanished into the darkness.

And then, suddenly—suddenly the man was standing right beside him. He was murmuring quietly into Tom's ear.

"You see, Tom, it's as I said. I just want for you what you want for yourself. And you know what that is, don't you?"

"No," said Tom weakly.

"Yes, you do," said the Lying Man. "You know what you really want." He chuckled softly. "Death, Tom. That's it, isn't it? You don't want to come out of this coma at all, do you? Why should you? Your life isn't worth living. Of course you want to die. You want to die."

Horrified, Tom turned to him quickly. The Lying Man smiled, his expression seemingly full of kindness. But his eyes! His eyes were dancing with the raging electric power of his absolute wickedness.

"And now," said the Lying Man, "we're both going to get what we want!"

The next moment he was gone—all of him was gone, that is, except his laughter. His laughter continued to trail back to Tom out of the shadows, fading only slowly.

And as the laughter faded, a new noise replaced it. Soft at first. A steady, rhythmic pounding. It was coming from upstairs.

Tom listened. The thudding went on. It grew louder. Now and then it was punctuated by high, hollow shrieks that drifted like ghostly echoes down the stairs, down the hall, to where Tom stood.

The malevolents!

Tom's eyes widened as he lifted his gaze to the ceiling.

Moment by moment, the pounding upstairs became more insistent. The shrieks became wilder, more ravenous.

Of course. He had forgotten. The Lying Man was the master of the malevolents. The Lying Man was the King of Death. He had kept Tom here, delayed him, stalled him with his talk while the fog climbed up the hill outside, while the malevolents advanced on the school.

And Tom, heartbroken and confused, weak with sorrow, had listened to him. Had stood here. Had given the malevolents the time they needed to make their approach.

And now they were here. Pounding on the windows. Shrieking for entry.

Hungry for Tom's life.

23.

The pounding grew steadily louder. Those strange echoing shrieks grew louder. And now there were other noises. A crack. A spatter.

Glass breaking. The windows were giving way.

Fear flowed into Tom like electricity, jolting him out of his weakness, jolting him out of his sorrowing daze.

He heard the Lying Man whisper in his mind:

I want for you what you want for yourself. Death. You want to die.

Was it true? He was so confused now, so unhappy, so incredibly weary of fighting his way through this nightmare, that he didn't know what was true anymore or whom to trust. But he *wanted* to know. He still had that—that curiosity to know the truth that drove him on, that wouldn't let him give up.

You want to die, the Lying Man insisted.

And Tom thought: *No. No, I don't. Not yet, at least.*

He was still a reporter, after all. He couldn't die before he learned the rest of the story.

He hesitated another moment. He heard the malevolents trying to break in upstairs. He thought of their poisonous claws, their ravenous teeth. He remembered the lanky man with blond hair who had been dragged away screaming into the fog. He had cut his wrists, Lisa said. He had given in to despair. He really *had* wanted to die.

That's not me, Tom thought, fighting down the voice of the Lying Man. *That's not going to be me.*

He gripped his bat tightly and started to run.

He dashed through the darkness of the halls. Whispers trailed past him like wind. Shadows dashed by on every side of him. Memories. The haunting memories he had wanted to leave behind. Pulling at him. Calling to him.

He reached the bottom of the stairway. Looked up into the dim, gray light above. Not much light—just the light leaking down the hall from the lobby windows—but enough to make his way by. The pounding up there continued. The shrieking continued. They would break through soon. He had to hurry.

He started up, taking the stairs two and three at a time.

It was not fast enough.

As he reached the top of the flight, he heard a tremendous shattering noise. He peered down the hall, through the shadows, into the brighter light of the lobby. He saw that two of the windows had already broken, their shards and splinters glittering on the floor in the gray light. Now, even as he watched, thunder crashed and lightning flickered and another window exploded and then another. The wind brought the rain lashing in through the openings. More lightning. More thunder. And then the fog tumbled into the corridor.

And the malevolents came with it.

Lit by the flickering blasts of light, the monsters climbed through the broken windows, fighting with one another to be the first in. They tore at one another's rotting piebald flesh with their toxic claws. The jagged broken glass tore at them, too. They screamed—and their horrible screams were lost beneath the wild, raging thunder. But nothing slowed them down. Nothing stopped them. As the mist hissed into the school, as the wind-whipped rain drenched the glass-strewn floor, as the thunder and lightning rocked the school and lit the corridor, the malevolents tumbled through the windows, staggering across the hall, sniffing the air and eyeing the darkness, searching for their prey.

There was no chance of getting past them. No chance of fighting so many. Tom had to find another way out.

He turned and looked away from the lobby, down the other hall. At the rear of the school, there were doors leading onto the athletic fields. Maybe there was still a chance he could reach them before the fog surrounded the school entirely. He could cross the fields and climb the fence and make his way to town, to Pinewood Lane, to Karen Lee.

Panting, terrified, he left the lobby of monsters behind and took off down the hall to the back of the school at top speed. Yet, even now, even in his fear, he was aware of the heaviness and confusion inside him.

Look at yourself, Tom. Really look at yourself for a change. Look at your life. You've lost your brother. You've lost your friends. You've spent years pining for a girl who despises you . . .

He knew that heaviness was slowing him down, making him weak. He knew he had to fight against it.

Despair is not an option.

He gritted his teeth. Pushed himself on, racing headlong down the hall.

There they were: the double doors that led to the fields

in back. There were no windows here, so he couldn't check the conditions outside. He didn't know what he was about to find. He didn't know what he was charging into. But he had to try it.

He flung himself against the doors. Hit the bar of the doors with his shoulder and shoved it open, tumbling after it out of the school, into the back fields.

He tumbled into a tempest. The storm out here was raging full blast, the power of it almost unbelievable. The sky was flashing continuously. The thunder cracked and muttered and rolled. The wind lashed at his face and the rain pounded him.

But there was no fog. There were no malevolents. Through the streaming gray downpour, he could see across the playing fields to the horizon.

He headed in that direction—he tried to, anyway. He got three steps, and then the wind strengthened even more, hammering against him without ceasing. He fought forward another step, but the wind was overpowering. The rain whipped his face painfully. He had to raise his arm to protect his eyes.

As he stood there, trying to battle the wind, there was a flash of lightning and a blast of thunder so loud it deafened him. He felt the earth tremble beneath his feet, shake so hard he was afraid it would open up and swallow him.

He had never felt a storm like this—it seemed beyond the bounds of nature.

For a moment, the noise trembled lower, but it seemed to Tom it wasn't fading but only gathering for some greater blast.

And then it came. A crackling flash of lightning like no lightning there had ever been, a supernatural explosion of radiance that blinded him and a crash of thunder that swallowed every other sound. The wind grew even stronger. The rain fell even harder. It seemed he was being spun and lifted and carried away by a whipping whirlpool of light and sound and air and pain. It was as if the chaos in his heart had overflowed into the chaos around him and the chaos around him had engulfed all the world.

Everything turned gray as the tempest overwhelmed him. There was nothing left anywhere except the storm.

PART III

MURDER AT THE MONASTERY

24.

The rain fell steadily. Drenched and weary, Tom trudged up a steep two-lane road. He moved in the shadows of overhanging oak and eucalyptus trees, the cold downpour dripping on him from their leaves.

He looked around, bewildered. It was strange—very strange: he couldn't remember how he had gotten here. He had stepped out of the school into a raging storm—he remembered that. And he remembered the wind and the lightning and thunder—the incredible intensity of them. But then . . . ? There was nothing after that. He was just suddenly here. It was as if there had been some weird skip in the video of his life, a missing transition.

And now? He wasn't sure. Something felt wrong. Something felt different and strange. He couldn't quite tell what it was, but he sensed he had entered a new phase of this nightmare.

He trudged on beneath the dripping trees, nearing the top of the hill. From there, he would be able to look down onto the main street of town, Route 190. There would be a little strip of stores, gas stations, and restaurants. The freeway to the right, and the ocean beyond. The high hills to the left, dotted with houses.

A few yards from the crest, Tom stopped. He had heard something. A sort of steady *whoosh* and whisper. He realized he had been hearing it for some time, but he hadn't noticed it before because it blended in with the background and because . . . well, because it was so normal. He was used to hearing it every day.

It was the sound of cars on the freeway.

Tom's lips parted in surprise as he realized this. This was what he'd been missing all this time—all this time he'd been in this bizarre coma-world. The noise of freeway traffic, the songs of birds, the presence of other people. The normal sounds and movements of life. Had they all come back now? What did it mean?

He started walking again, faster, covering the last few yards to the peak of the hill.

He stopped at the crest and looked down into the center of town. A feeling of wonder and hope spread through him. Sure enough, there were cars passing on the freeway down there, just as there usually were. There were cars on 190, too. Cars pausing at the stoplight, moving on when the light turned green. Cars pulling into the diagonal spaces outside the shops and restaurants. Cars stopping at the pump for gas. Just like always.

Another movement caught Tom's attention and he turned and saw, to his amazement, an actual pedestrian, a sure-enough ordinary normal human being, big as life. It was a woman with a shopping bag coming out of the Easy Mart at the Shell station, heading for her parked SUV. Tom stared at her with wonder, as if she were an angel descended from heaven. And then . . .

Then Tom lifted his eyes and he saw the Pacific. What a wonderful sight it was! The ocean was dark and churning under the gray sky, its waves rising to meet the rain, its white-caps snapping at the clouds. But the best part was: there was no fog, no marine layer. In fact, now that he thought about it, there was no sign of fog anywhere. No malevolents.

Did that mean he had finally escaped them? Was he getting better? Was he going to live and regain consciousness?

His excitement rose as he started down the hill.

He entered the heart of Springland. He passed the Greenhouse Restaurant on his left. He could see people through the windows of the green clapboard building: more ordinary people sitting at the tables in there eating and talking. He could see people through the window of the antique shop, too. And more people pulling into the Shell station in their cars. It was as if he had returned to the land of the living after a long journey through a barren nightmare.

Just as he reached the corner, a tall, weathered ranchhand came out of the hardware store and moved past Tom toward a black pickup parked at the curb. Tom smiled a greeting at the man, eager to talk to someone, to anyone.

"Hey. How goes it?" Tom said.

The ranchhand took no notice of him. He walked past Tom as if he weren't there. Got into his truck. Drove away.

Tom sighed. He had wanted so much to hear another human voice, a real, normal human voice. After the ranchhand was gone, he stood on the corner for a second, looking around for someone else to talk to. But there was no one nearby. The rain continued to drench him. His soaked, clammy clothes clung to him uncomfortably. He had to move on. He had to get to 47 Pinewood Lane. The Pinewood

Apartments. That's why he was here. To find Karen Lee, the woman in the white blouse. To hear what it was she so desperately wanted to tell him. The truth he could not remember.

The building called Pinewood Apartments was the only high-rise in town. Tom could see it from here: a white six-story building embedded precariously in the slope of the hills above him, with balconies on every floor overlooking the freeway and the sea.

Tom started toward it, up the road through the rain.

Then suddenly he was standing outside the building. Again, he couldn't remember how he had gotten here. He had begun walking and then there was a kind of *fritz*—like static or something—and suddenly he was just here, looking in through the glass doors that led to the building's lobby. Very freaky. Very strange.

He shook his head, like a dog shaking off water. He was tired, that's all. Zoning out. He ran his fingers through his hair, combing out the rain. Once he found Karen Lee, things would start to make more sense. *Just tired*, he told himself again.

Now he was in the lobby. He didn't remember pushing through the doors, but he must have. He was standing just inside, in a broad open space with both an elevator and a flight of stairs leading upward. There was a semicircular desk in the center. A receptionist stood behind it, a woman of maybe thirty or so. She had long black hair and a severe expression on her face. She looked, Tom thought, like an angry schoolteacher. She stood still, staring sternly at him as if she were about to scold him for not paying attention in class.

He walked toward her.

"Hi. My name is Tom Harding," he said. "I'm here to see Karen Lee in 6B."

The woman went on staring at him—staring and frowning. She didn't seem to approve of him. She wouldn't even answer.

"Excuse me?" said Tom. "Hello? I'd like to see Miss Lee in 6B."

Still—no response. Tom felt a weird little charge of anxiety. He remembered the ranchhand who had walked right past him as if he weren't there. A cold feeling went down his neck, as if someone had put a piece of ice against his skin.

"Miss?" he said out loud to the frowning woman at the reception desk. He waved his hand in front of her face. "Miss, can you hear me?"

And still, the woman didn't move, didn't answer. Her eyes shifted a little, and Tom realized with a jolt that she wasn't really looking at him at all. She was looking through him, as if she didn't see him, as if he were invisible to her, as if he were . . .

. . . a ghost.

The thought came into Tom's mind before he could stop it: *Am I a ghost? Am I dead? Am I already dead?*

Just then the phone on the reception desk rang. Immediately the woman behind the desk responded, picked it up.

"Front desk," she said in a brisk voice.

She turned her back on Tom and went on talking into the phone.

It was true! She couldn't see him, couldn't hear him at all!

Tom raised his hands to touch his own chest, as if he might find he had become insubstantial, a phantom. The receptionist went on talking into the phone, oblivious to his presence.

Tom's anxiety turned to fear. Desperate to prove himself wrong, he moved away from the receptionist. Moved to the elevators. He pressed the Up button. The elevator didn't light up. Didn't move.

Of course not.

Because ghosts can't call elevators, Tom thought.

No, no, no, that couldn't be right. The elevator was probably broken. He looked around. The stairs. He would use the stairs. He rushed over to them. The receptionist didn't try to stop him from going up.

Right. Because she doesn't even know I'm here.

He climbed the stairs quickly with the question repeating and repeating itself in his mind. *Did I die? Was that storm the end of me? Am I dead? Am I already dead?*

Out of breath, he reached the sixth-floor landing. Karen Lee's apartment, 6B, was down at the end of the hall. He hurried to it. Knocked at the door. Noticed a doorbell button. Pressed it. He didn't hear any bell ring.

Of course not.

He knocked again. He called out. "Miss Lee? It's Tom Harding. From the *Sentinel*." No answer. He pounded loudly on the door with his fist. "Miss Lee?"

Panic was rising in him. *Am I dead? Am I already dead?* He drew back his hand to pound on the door again. But before he could, he heard sounds behind him. A soft *clunk*. A *whir*.

He turned around. It was the elevator. It was on the move.

It wasn't broken, then. He took a few cautious steps down the hall until he could see the numbers above the elevator door. Sure enough, the light was flashing from one number to another as the elevator climbed, from two to three to four. Five. Six.

Tom moved closer. He was right in front of the elevator when it stopped. He was standing and watching as the door slid open.

He could not believe what he saw inside. He gaped wild-eyed, letting out his breath in a single rush.

Tom Harding stood and stared in fear and amazement as Tom Harding stepped out of the elevator into the hall.

25.

A double of himself! A doppelgänger!

Tom would not have thought anything could have frightened him more than he had been frightened already on this terrible day. He did not think anything could have raised in him the sheer terror he had felt when the malevolents broke into his house or could have chilled him the way the ghosts of his memory had in the school. He did not think anything could make his heart turn to ice the way it had when he had looked into the wicked eyes of the Lying Man.

But this was worse than any of that. This was scarier by far.

The sight of his own double made him feel as if his very soul had been stolen from him. His very essence, his very self. Because if this—this *thing* stepping out of the elevator—if this was Tom Harding, then who was he? What was happening to him?

The doppelgänger came walking toward him—right toward him, as if it didn't see him standing there. Before Tom realized what was going to happen, before he could react and get out of the way, his double reached him and walked into him—and then *walked right through him*!

It was the worst thing Tom had ever felt—worse even than the moment when the malevolents had fallen on him. It was *sicker* than that. The double broke through the boundaries of Tom's being and Tom felt for a moment that he had become nothing, that he had exploded into atoms and blown away. For an instant, he had no sense of himself, no memory, no presence. For an instant, he was the double and the double was him.

Then it was over. The doppelgänger had passed through him. Tom felt himself come into being again. Only then, with a nauseating shock, did he remember the momentary, sickening sensation of nothingness.

Unsteady, he turned and watched as the doppelgänger continued down the hall as if nothing had happened.

The double approached the door of 6B. He knocked softly. Immediately, a voice Tom recognized, Karen Lee's voice, answered from within.

"Who is it?"

"It's Tom," said the double. "It's Tom Harding from the *Sentinel*."

You're not! Tom wanted to shout at him. *You're not Tom Harding! I am!*

But he didn't shout. He didn't say anything. He wasn't sure anymore who he was or what was real or what was true. All he could do was stand there, gaping in silence, as the apartment door slowly opened.

Karen Lee looked out at the doppelgänger. Tom recognized her at once. She was the woman in the white blouse who had stood in his driveway. A small, thin woman about forty or so. Her eyes shifted nervously past the double. She looked down the hall as if she was worried someone else was hiding behind him. Her gaze passed over Tom but didn't pause. She didn't see him. She turned back to his double. She spoke to him in a low, rapid voice, almost a whisper.

"I made a mistake," she said. "I'm sorry, but you have to go."

"But you were the one who called me," the doppelgänger answered, looking confused. "You told me I should come."

"I . . . I was wrong," said the woman. "I don't know what I was thinking. I don't want you here. You have to go."

She's afraid, Tom thought as he watched them. And he urged his double in his mind: *Don't leave. Stand your ground. Help her.*

The double seemed to obey. "It sounded like it was important," he said. "It sounded like you really needed to talk to me."

"I'm telling you," said Karen Lee urgently, "I can't. Please. Just go away."

She started to close the door. Watching the scene, Tom thought: *Don't let her do it. Something's wrong. Find out what it is.*

And, as if the doppelgänger could hear him, he put his hand out, stopping the door, holding it open for a second.

"Wait," he said. "Please don't. I can see something's the matter. You're afraid. Let me help you."

Karen Lee hesitated, doubtful. "You can't. You don't know what you're getting into."

"Then tell me," said Tom's doppelgänger. "I can't do anything if I don't know what you're talking about."

Karen Lee looked at him through the gap in the door. The fear was plain in her eyes. Tom's double let his hand fall—he couldn't force her to let him in if she didn't want to. It had to be her decision.

Karen Lee and the doppelgänger stood face-to-face at the half-opened door. Tom watched them in that moment of decision—and all at once, he realized: he knew what was going to happen next. Sure he did. He had lived through this scene already. It was his memory. But it was different from the memories he had seen at the school. Those memories had been ghosts. This one was real—more real than he was. It was he who was the ghost!

Karen Lee hesitated one more moment. Then, as Tom knew she would, she pulled the door open all the way.

"Come in. Quickly," she said. "Before someone sees you."

The Tom doppelgänger stepped inside the apartment. Tom himself hurried forward, hoping to slip in behind him. But before he could reach her, Karen Lee shut the door in his face.

Oh no, thought Tom.

Then—another *fritz*—another skip in the memory video—and Tom was inside the apartment, just like that. He didn't know how it had happened. He didn't feel he had passed through the door or anything. He was just suddenly there, that's all. Standing there like an unseen specter while his own double and Karen Lee confronted each other.

Stunned, Tom looked around—and the doppelgänger

looked around—and they saw that the apartment was in shambles.

"He came here," said Karen Lee. "It was like he was insane."

The chairs were all turned over on their sides. A lampstand lay toppled. Its lamp lay broken beside it amid a sprinkling of shattered glass. The curtains had been torn off the windows and lay in a pile on the floor, the curtain rods broken on top of them.

"He asked me if I was going to tell," said Karen Lee. "I told him I didn't know, I wasn't sure. But I think he could see the truth in my eyes. He offered me money to stay quiet . . . but when I wouldn't take it, he just . . . he went crazy. Lost his temper. He said he wouldn't let me destroy him and his family. He would hurt me, he said. He said he would kill me if he had to. I was so scared . . . I promised to keep my mouth shut, but . . . I just can't . . ." She made a noise, covered her mouth with her hand and started to cry. "I can't keep quiet anymore."

The Tom double stood there awkwardly, not knowing what to do, how to comfort her. Tom himself, in a gesture of kindness, moved to where the lampstand was lying. He crouched down and reached to pick it up. His fingers closed on the wooden shaft of it—and they went right through!

The sight was such a shock that Tom tried again. Same deal. He couldn't grip the lamp. He couldn't touch it.

I'm fading, he thought. *I'm fading away.*

He stood up. The doppelgänger came toward him. Afraid he would pass through him again—afraid of that awful feeling of nothingness—Tom moved quickly out of his way. He watched as the double did just what he had done. He crouched down, too. He took hold of the lampstand. He gripped it, lifted it, as Tom had tried to. He set it right. The doppelgänger could do it and he couldn't.

I'm fading away to nothing. Soon I won't exist at all.

The double looked at Karen Lee as she cried. "You should call the police," he told her.

She shook her head. "He has friends on the police force. He has friends everywhere. A lot of them. Powerful people. I don't know who to trust."

Tom's double nodded. "You can trust me," he said. "Once I write the story, once it's public, he won't be able to do anything to you. If he does, everyone will know it's him. Who is he? What is he trying to keep secret?"

Karen Lee stared at the doppelgänger, her eyes bright through the tears. Tom could see she desperately wanted to speak, to tell the truth. She forced the words out.

"He was the one who sold drugs to the team," she said. "I'm his receptionist and assistant. I saw everything. The coach—Coach Petrie—he would come to him after hours at the office. He brought him cash, and the doctor gave him hypodermics full of steroids. And pills to take, too. He told me if I told anyone about it, I would go to prison, the same as him. So I was scared. I kept my mouth shut. I kept it secret for three years. But then—then when I heard about your story in the school newspaper, I realized I'd been wrong. I should've told at the start. I shouldn't have stood by and let it happen. I told him: They're going to catch us eventually. We should do the right thing. We should tell the truth. Maybe that way the law won't be so hard on us. But he . . . he got upset. And then he came here. Threatened me . . ."

Watching Karen Lee—watching the doppelgänger— Tom felt his heart sinking inside him. He knew what was going to happen next, what they would both say next. He remembered. He even remembered the shock he felt the first time he heard it. He didn't want to hear it again. He didn't want to be here anymore.

But he stayed where he was. He stood and listened. He had looked too hard for the answers to run away from them now.

"Who was this?" said Tom's double. "Who sold the players the drugs? Who threatened you like this?"

Karen Lee, still crying, whispered the name: "Dr. Cameron."

26.

The next moment was beyond belief. Tom saw it happen with his own eyes and still couldn't take it in, couldn't get his mind to grasp it.

"Dr. Cameron," said Karen Lee—and Tom's double straightened in surprise. *Dr. Cameron? Marie's father!* The double began to step back . . . and then stopped. No, he didn't stop. He *froze*. He froze completely in mid-step, his foot half lifted off the floor. Before Tom fully comprehended what he was seeing, his gaze shifted to Karen Lee and he saw that she, too, had gone utterly motionless. She was standing unblinking, with her lips still parted on the name of Marie's father.

Tom looked around him. The apartment was silent. It was not an ordinary silence. It was complete. Nothing disturbed it. The refrigerator wasn't humming. There were no voices from other apartments or from outside. The air itself seemed to have stopped moving entirely.

Tom stared at Karen Lee. He stared at his double. He moved to his double and looked right into his face—right into his own face—and yet the doppelgänger did not budge. Quickly, Tom went around him. He went to the glass doors that led out onto the balcony. He looked through.

The rain was motionless in the sky. It streaked the air but didn't fall. Stupefied, Tom looked down the hill. He saw the cars on the town's main street. They were no longer moving either. Beyond that, he saw the ocean, saw that the Pacific itself had ceased all motion. Its waves did not rise and fall but were frozen at their crests, reaching up toward the low clouds, which likewise did not so much as shift in the sky.

His eyes wide, Tom spun back to the scene in the apartment. It was just as it had been. Tom's double stepping back in shock. Karen Lee locked in the instant after she had spoken. A scene so uncanny, it filled Tom with a sense of helplessness, not to mention fear. A million explanations began to form in his mind, but each trailed off unfinished. Because nothing explained it. It was impossible.

Tom glanced out the glass doors again. The rain still hung midair, forever falling from motionless clouds onto a still ocean. But something was different. Something had changed. It took Tom a moment, but then he realized what it was.

The sky was darker now than it had been a moment before. The whole scene was darker. The light had faded. And as Tom stood there staring at the bizarrely motionless view, the scene grew even darker still.

He faced the apartment again and, yes, here, too, the light was going out. It was as if night was falling. Every second that passed, the frozen world turned a deeper gray. Soon, Tom realized, very soon, all the light would be gone. There would be blackness.

Tom took a slow, hesitant step away from the glass doors, back toward his own frozen double. Now, finally, an idea was beginning to take shape in his mind, the beginning of an explanation. Maybe this, he thought—this frozen moment—was the place where his memory ended. He'd heard that happened to people sometimes when they were in an accident or got injured—or got shot. The memory of the trauma was erased. The shock was too much to bear and the brain shut down. Maybe this was that moment. Maybe, in fighting his way to the school, he had unlocked everything that remained in his memory, and this was as far as he could go.

He had come this far through the dangerous world of his imagination, but he had reached the end. The darkness was falling now because there was nothing after this. Only blackness. Unconsciousness. Coma—endless coma until his heart stopped and his life was over.

Unless . . .

Unless what? What could he do? Moment by moment, the apartment grew even darker. Already it seemed a sort of dusk had settled over the scene. When the darkness was complete there would be nowhere else to go, nothing to think about . . . nothing.

Tom lifted his hand uncertainly. It was growing dim in front of him. He himself was fading into the darkness. Slowly, tentatively, he reached out toward his double. He extended his hand toward the doppelgänger's shoulder and then—then, holding his breath, he pushed it through.

As if it were made of smoke, his hand seemed to dissipate and vanish in front of Tom's eyes. It went right into the double's shoulder, and Tom gave a groan as he felt the beginning of that horrible nothingness again, that sensation of atomizing he had felt out in the hall.

And yet maybe there was a chance, just a chance, that that was exactly what could save him.

An even deeper darkness than evening now folded over the scene. Tom knew his wounded mind could not remember anymore.

But what if, he thought—*what if instead of remembering, I could relive it?*

It might work. It might. If he could enter his doppelgänger before the darkness fell—lose himself in his double as he had for that one second out in the hall—maybe he could relive the events that had plunged him into this coma-world in the first place. Somewhere in his brain those events were recorded, after all, even if his memory couldn't access them. But if he could *become* his memory, then maybe he could force himself to face the thoughts and feelings and events— the suffering—that had brought him here, and that were keeping him from making his way back into the light of life.

It was a frightening prospect. He knew if he went through with it, the Tom he was now would vanish. If he entered into the doppelgänger, if he became one with his memory, he would no longer know that he was in a coma. He would no longer know that this was his imagination. He would be back in the life that had brought him here, and he would no longer know what was going to happen next.

He was going to have to relive the worst moments of his

life—the last moments of his life—as if they were happening for the first time. It was the only way he could overcome his mind's resistance and discover the whole truth.

He was going to have to see it with his own eyes.

The double stood frozen. Karen Lee stood frozen. The world stood frozen. And night fell steadily. The darkness was almost complete.

Tom had to choose—and fast. He had to decide right now which he wanted more, the painless comfort of unconsciousness or the agony of knowing.

It's like the Bible says, he remembered Lisa telling him. *Find the truth—and the truth will set you free.*

Well, he answered in his mind, *the truth is what I'm here for.*

And as the darkness fell around him, he stepped forward boldly. He walked into the body of his doppelgänger. Directly into nothingness. Directly into the moment of his own destruction.

27.

D r. Cameron," said Karen Lee.

Tom was so shocked by the words he took a step backward.

"Dr. Cameron? But that's not poss—" he started to say. He had been about to protest that it couldn't be true, it couldn't have been Dr. Cameron who had sold the drugs to the football players. It couldn't have been Marie's decent, sophisticated, well-spoken father—the man who served on so many boards of so many charities, the man who had his picture taken with so many powerful, famous people. He couldn't be the one who had exchanged injections and pills for fistfuls of cash. Who had come here and threatened Karen Lee and violently torn her apartment to pieces.

But the protest died in his mouth. He knew deep down that Karen Lee was telling the truth. Dr. Cameron's guilt would explain a lot. It would explain what Marie had been saying to Gordon in the gym. She and her father had been trying to make a friend of Tom so they could convince him to stop looking for the rest of the story about the championship Tigers. They thought if Tom liked Dr. Cameron enough— and if he thought he had a chance to win Marie—they might be able to convince him to leave the story alone, to keep Dr. Cameron's guilt out of the newspaper.

Oh, come on, baby, he could imagine Marie saying to him. In that same irresistible coaxing tone she had used on Gordon. *Just do it for me.*

Tom took a deep breath. He reached into his pocket and took out his phone. There was a recorder function on it. He pressed the button. He held the phone out toward Karen Lee.

"Miss Lee," he said. "Tell me the story. Tell me the whole story from the beginning."

Karen Lee's tears were subsiding. "All right," she said with a weary nod. "I can't keep it secret anymore."

———

Twenty minutes later Tom had it all, the whole story recorded on his phone.

Dr. Cameron—Karen Lee told him—loved being an important man. He loved being appointed to boards, loved having his picture taken with politicians and celebrities. But that way of life cost a lot of money, more money than he made in his medical practice. So he had begun making risky investments in the stock market, hoping the large returns would allow him to live at that high level that made him feel important.

When the market suddenly dropped, his money dried up. Dr. Cameron went into debt, deep into debt. But instead of cutting back on his spending, instead of sacrificing his wealthy life and his pride, he began to borrow—to borrow a lot—from the banks, at first, and then, when the banks wouldn't lend him any more, from loan sharks, mobster thugs from Nevada who charged insanely high interest and demanded to be paid every week or else.

The further into debt Dr. Cameron went, the more risks he took in the market, hoping to hit it big and get free from the mobsters' clutches. The more risks he took, the deeper into debt he went: a vicious cycle. Soon the thugs were threatening him—threatening his wife—threatening his children. If he couldn't pay back the money, they said, he would have to pay them back in other ways: by supplying them with prescription drugs that they could resell on the black market.

So now the respectable doctor had become a criminal, a drug dealer.

Dr. Cameron was desperate to get out, desperate to get free of his troubles. And he thought he saw a way. Coach Petrie was one of his patients. The doctor suggested he could help the Tigers play better, ensure they would start winning. He said he could give them a chance to make it all the way to the Open Division and take the state trophy. Coach decided it was worth a try. He was soon visiting the doctor's office more and more often, buying more and more of the illegal performance enhancers that gave his players extra size and strength. The Tigers started winning—against all odds, against all expectations—and Dr. Cameron started using his drug profits to bet on the final outcome of the championship with the bookies in Vegas. The odds against the Tigers at that early stage were enormous. If the Tigers won it all, the bookies would have to pay off big. Dr. Cameron could get out of debt at last.

It was no wonder Dr. Cameron was so frightened his story would come out. If his role in the Tigers' corruption became public, all his criminal dealings would be exposed.

Not only would he be sent to prison for a long time, but there'd be some very angry thugs in Nevada, tough guys who felt he'd ripped them off by rigging the big game without telling them.

His life—his honor, his importance, his friendships with governors and mayors and celebrities—it would all come crashing down in ruin and disgrace.

Karen Lee had been on hand as much of this tragedy unfolded. She had witnessed some of it and overheard some, and Dr. Cameron, in his misery, had even confided some of it to her. But she'd been afraid to tell anyone—afraid she would get in trouble herself and afraid of the lengths to which Dr. Cameron would go to silence her. She had kept her secrets for three years—right up until she had read Tom's story in the paper. Then the quiet promptings of her conscience had grown louder and she could no longer resist them. Before calling Tom, she had tried to convince Dr. Cameron to come forward with the truth himself. But he had refused—and then, later, he had come to her apartment and tried to terrorize her into keeping her long silence.

———

As Tom walked out of apartment 6B, he realized he was walking into a world of trouble. The *Sentinel* story about the Tigers' drug use had already caused a firestorm of controversy. If he and Lisa ran this additional story about Dr. Cameron's involvement, the turmoil would grow tenfold. They would not only be accusing one of the most important men in town of breaking the law. They'd be uncovering a world of corruption and drug deals that could have repercussions through the whole city, maybe the whole state. A lot of people—Dr. Cameron, Coach Petrie, and all their important friends and supporters—would do anything they could to stop Tom and Lisa, to shut them up and shut them down.

So Tom knew he needed to act fast. Once the story was in the newspaper, once everyone knew the truth, Dr. Cameron wouldn't dare attack Karen Lee again. And any important friends he had would probably turn tail and run instead of helping him. They wouldn't want to risk getting in trouble themselves.

Tom's heart was beating hard as he rode the elevator down to the lobby. Thoughts were crowding into his mind. He had to call Lisa. They had to get to work as quickly as they could. Write the story, put the paper out before anyone could stop them.

Marie will never forgive me, he thought. *She will hate me forever.*

He tried to push the idea out of his mind. What difference did it make whether Marie hated him or not? All her affection for him had been a lie anyway. He couldn't lose a girl he'd never really had.

But even as he told himself that, the image of her face came to him. That amazingly pretty face he had loved since he was a little kid. The idea that she might hate him forever hurt—it hurt more than he wanted to admit. And he had a feeling it was going to hurt for a long, long time to come.

The elevator stopped. The door opened. Tom stepped out into the lobby. The receptionist with the stern face flashed a brief smile at him from behind her desk.

"Have a nice day," she said without much feeling.

Tom nodded and walked out of the building.

The rain had slowed to a drizzle now. Tom's Mustang was parked across the street. He got into it, turned on the engine, turned on the windshield wipers. As the wipers swept the rain off the glass, he dug his phone out of his pocket again. He called up Lisa's name on his speed dial.

But before he could press the Call button, the phone rang. The readout lit up: *Marie Cameron*.

Tom stared at the name for only a second. Then he answered.

"It's me, Tom," she said.

The sweet, soft voice seemed to pierce through him. "Marie." Her name came out of him in a low murmur. This was probably the last time she would ever speak to him, he realized.

"I need to talk to you, Tom," she said. "It's important."

Holding the phone to his ear, Tom looked out the windshield at the street in front of him, looked through the air gray with rain. "Go ahead," he said.

"Not on the phone. We have to meet. It's about . . . it's about my dad."

"Your dad?"

"Yes. And about the football team. My dad was the one who . . . Look, I don't want to say it on the phone. Please . . ."

Tom was quiet a moment, surprised. This was a twist. It didn't make sense. If Marie had been flirting with him to keep him from finding out the truth, why was she telling it to him straight out like this? "I already know about that," he said. "And listen, I'm sorry. I wish I could keep quiet about it."

"Keep quiet?" said Marie, sounding startled. "No, no, you can't keep quiet. Of course not. You have to write about it in the paper. But you can't write about it until you know the whole story. The real story."

Now Tom was just plain confused. "What do you mean?"

"It's not what you think, Tom. It's totally different than what it sounds like. Believe me. You have to meet me. Somewhere secret. I don't want my father to know. Or Gordon."

"Gordon? What's he got to do with it?"

"Tom," said Marie—and again, her voice seemed to go right into him. "I promise I'll tell you everything if you just meet me."

Tom only hesitated another moment. What could he do? He had to meet her. Maybe she was right. Maybe he didn't know the whole story. Before he did anything else, he had to find out all the facts.

"Okay," he said quietly. "Where do you want to meet?"

"Up on Cold Water Mountain," Marie answered. "No one goes there since the fire. Meet me at the monastery."

28.

t was a ten-minute drive to the trailhead. Half an hour's hike up into the hills. Soon Tom was moving through the part of the woods that had been destroyed last summer by the Independence Fire. The blaze had started after a bunch of kids set off some fireworks near the trail. The dry summer brush had been torched, and the flames had swept through the woods for nearly three days before the firemen had finally managed to put the fire out. It had left behind a hellish landscape: a whole forest of twisted, blackened trees, their gnarled branches stunted, their broken silhouettes twisted against the boiling, cloud-covered sky.

The rain had stopped, but the light was failing. Evening was spreading across the mountainside like a gray stain. Tendrils of mist twined among the spooky, corkscrewing, coal-black corpses that had once been living trees.

Tom's footsteps were the only noises in the deserted place. They were eerily loud as he made his way along the trail, under the gnarled branches. It was not long before the charred timbers of the monastery roof became visible over the ridge. A few more steps and the rest of the retreat came into view.

Santa Maria had been a retreat for Catholic monks who wanted to get away from the world and contemplate God. Most of the monks came up from the main monastery building in the town below, but others came from around the country, too, to see the artwork here and to appreciate the beautiful views of the mountainside and the ocean. The place had actually been kind of famous for a while. But it was just a ruin now. Jagged, fire-blackened walls stood against the backdrop of the distant sea. There were piles of toppled bricks. A stone chimney still standing lopsided under a burned oak. Remnants of rooms with one or two walls remaining. Pieces of furniture—tables, chairs—burned and broken, lying in the dirt under the burned, broken trees as if they were part of the forest as well.

Just beyond the building site, there was a huge table of rock jutting out from the side of the mountain. It formed a sort of natural balcony, beyond which Tom could see the town spread out among the trees below, and the ocean, endless and dark blue under the churning gray sky. The monks had often come out onto this rock at the end of the day to watch the sunset.

Tom scanned the scene. Silent now. Motionless.

He called out, "Marie?"

But no one answered. Only the wind stirred, sending the high clouds tumbling and turning.

Debris crunched under his sneakers as he moved farther into the monastery site. He stepped out from behind the chimney and came into a room. It was the only room left standing here—almost intact, as if the fire somehow hadn't touched it. It had been the monastery chapel. The roof had burned off and one wall had crumbled to charcoal rubble. But three walls remained standing, scorched though they were. Some of the pews had survived as well, some toppled, some still in their rows, all of them scarred. The chapel crucifix seemed to have been melted into the wall behind the altar, but the shape of the cross remained there. The stained glass was all gone, but the peaked shapes of the windows were still visible high on the wall, open to the sky.

Tom stepped farther into the chapel, the grit on the floor jabbing up through his sneaker soles. He had the weird feeling that some ghostly presence was watching him—and then he understood why. On one of the walls, a heavy gilt picture frame hung askew. The painting in the frame had been burned away—all of it except one small jagged patch that held part of a face, the part with the eyes.

Tom felt a little chill. The eyes really did seem to be gazing at him through the gathering dusk. They were gentle eyes but full of pain. There was a line of blood running down the temple beside them. Maybe this had once been a picture of Jesus on the cross, Tom thought, or one of the suffering saints. He didn't know.

"It's sad to see this place in ruins," said a voice behind him.

Surprised, Tom spun around. Dr. Cameron was standing at the opening of the chapel, the place where the fourth wall had been before the fire destroyed it. The silver-blond-haired man with that perfect face so much like his daughter's looked relaxed and casual. He was wearing jeans and a sports jacket over a sweater, as if he had stopped off here on his way to a dinner out with friends. He smiled easily as Tom stood staring.

"You should see the look on your face," he said with a laugh. "You don't have to be so amazed. It's not like I'm a ghost or anything."

It was a moment before Tom could answer. Then he said, "I was expecting Marie."

"Yeah, I'll bet you were," Dr. Cameron said with another laugh, a harder laugh. "But I'm afraid I'm the best you're going to get."

Tom understood right away. Marie's phone call had just been more lies.

You have to write about it in the paper. But you can't write about it until you know the whole story. Meet me at the monastery.

He should've known. None of what she had said was true. She had just been doing her father's bidding. Tricking him into coming up here where there was no one to hear them, no one to see. Tom had been a fool for her from the beginning. Nothing had changed.

"I was worried that Ms. Lee might not be able to keep her mouth shut," Dr. Cameron went on. His footsteps crunched over the dirty floor as he came forward. "I paid the receptionist a few bucks to keep an eye on her for me. She told me you came by. I knew why."

"So you had your daughter call me and lure me up here," said Tom.

Dr. Cameron gave a full laugh, his white teeth gleaming in the darkening twilight. "Lure you! That's a sinister phrase! What do you think I am, some kind of gangster?"

Tom decided not to answer that.

"I just wanted a private place where we could talk," said Dr. Cameron. "I wanted to reason with you before you did something that could hurt a lot of people—and that might make your own life pretty difficult as well." He stopped advancing and stood still a few yards away from Tom. The gilt picture frame was on the wall between them. The suffering eyes that were all that was left of the painting seemed to watch them both. "Your choice is pretty simple, my friend. On the one hand, you write a story in the newspaper about me. You'll be pulling a thread that will unravel relationships throughout this town, throughout this state, even beyond that, and the repercussions will be enormous. You'll suffer. I'll suffer. A lot of important people will suffer. And Marie—Marie will suffer maybe more than anyone. If things go badly for me, her life will become"—he gestured at the burned-out walls around them—"a ruin, like this place. So that's one way you can go. The other way: you let me be your friend. I can help you—and your mom. There might be some money for you, for instance. You could use that, I'll bet. And I can help you get into a good college, get a good job. I have a lot of friends, Tom. Powerful friends. We can all help you."

Tom nodded. "If I agree to lie."

Dr. Cameron shrugged. "Nobody's asking you to lie. Not at all. I'm just asking you to use some discretion. Hold back. Don't write about me in your newspaper. Don't give people information they don't need, information that'll only do harm."

"Leaving stuff out is lying, too," said Tom. "Not telling the whole truth is lying."

Dr. Cameron smiled again. Looked down at his loafers. Shook his head. Looked up at Tom. "Have it your way. But here's how it is. If you tell the whole truth about me, you'll cause yourself and everyone else around you pain. If you . . . lie, as you say, I can give you so much. Money, contacts, success. The keys to the world. Don't be a fool, Tom. It's a good offer. It's everything. All you have to do is keep silent."

Tom hesitated for a moment before he answered. He knew Dr. Cameron was right. It was a good offer, as these things go. And maybe he should have felt tempted. But he didn't, not really. Money, contacts, success—sure, he wanted all that. But to lie in bed every night knowing he was nothing but a liar and a coward and a man who could be bought off—well, that didn't sound like having the keys to the world. That sounded like hell on earth.

A memory flitted through his mind then. Something Burt had told him once. Just a goofy piece of big brother–type advice he'd given him when they were both a lot younger, something about playing what Burt called the "bigger game." It was a long time ago now, one of Tom's birthdays. Burt had given him a baseball bat, Tom remembered, a Louisville Slugger Warrior. He still had that bat in his closet somewhere. Even though he never used it anymore, he wouldn't let his mother give it away . . .

"Tom?" said Dr. Cameron, breaking into his thoughts. "It's getting dark. I have a dinner engagement. I need an answer. Now."

"You know, my brother died in Afghanistan about six months ago," Tom said. It hurt him even now just to mention it. "He was helping evacuate some kids from a school that was in a danger zone. He was getting them to safety when a sniper shot him."

Dr. Cameron gave a puzzled gesture. "Yes, I heard. Too bad. But what's that got to do with anything?"

"It's just . . . He didn't have to be there, you know. He volunteered. He didn't have to. He could've gotten a job. Earned some money. Become a success in the world. He wanted that. He wanted all that stuff. All he had to do was stay home. Just stay home. But he was playing a bigger game."

"You're not making any sense," said Dr. Cameron.

"I'm not as brave as he was," Tom said, and his eyes got misty as he said it. "I'm not a hero like he was. But I'm playing that game, too. And you can keep your money, Dr. Cameron. And you can keep your important friends. And you can keep your daughter, if it comes to that. Because I'm going to write the truth about you, and nothing's going to stop me."

Dr. Cameron shook his head one more time. Then he put his hand in his jacket—and when he brought it out, he was holding a gun. The relaxed smile was gone from his face, and even in the growing darkness, his eyes gleamed with fury and hatred.

When Tom first saw the gun, he was surprised and frightened. Then he was not surprised. What was surprising about it? This was who Dr. Cameron was. This was what he had made himself. Tom stared into the weapon's deadly black bore and knew the doctor would pull the trigger without hesitation and that his life was over.

"You have a lot to learn, son," Dr. Cameron said. "Too bad you'll never get a chance to learn it. You want the truth? Here's the truth: this is what happens to people who can't keep their mouths shut."

It flashed through Tom's mind that he had to rush the man, had to try to get that gun from him—but there was no time for more than the thought. Because indeed Dr. Cameron did not hesitate. He pulled the trigger without conscience or remorse.

Tom never heard the explosion. He only felt the jolt of the bullet ripping into his flesh.

Then there was nothing but agony and darkness.

THE LAST INTERLUDE: THE WARRIOR

It was Tom's eleventh birthday. It had been a great day, a perfect spring day. He had had some friends over to the house for a party. Then, when the party was over, Burt had given him his last present. It was an aluminum baseball bat. A Louisville Slugger Warrior. Burt had wrapped it up in some red paper, but of course he couldn't disguise the shape of it. It was obvious what it was. Burt handed the long cylinder to Tom and said, "Here, kid. It's a sweater." Which had seemed hilarious at the time.

The next day was a Sunday. In the afternoon after church, Burt took him to the park and pitched to him. He gave him some tips on his swing, told him how to choke up late in the count. After about an hour, Tom could tell that the lesson had worked. He was whacking the ball better than he ever had, hitting solid singles right over Burt's head, plus a couple of blasts that would have definitely earned him extra bases in a real game.

"You can be a big hitter if you work at it," Burt said as

they walked home from the park. The light of the long day was dying as the sun went down toward the ocean.

Tom shrugged. "We play in school sometimes, but it's not much fun."

"What do you mean?" Burt asked, surprised. "You don't like baseball?"

"Not the way Mrs. Lerner plays it. She won't let us keep score."

"Oh yeah," said Burt with a laugh, "I remember Mrs. Lerner." He did a comical, high-pitched Mrs. Lerner voice that made Tom laugh, too. "'It doesn't matter who wins, children. If you don't try to win, you won't feel bad when you lose.'"

"That's her, all right," said Tom. "She makes the game boring."

"Well, yeah. 'Cause, I mean, that's what a game is all about, right? It's about trying to win. When you're in a game, you should try to win with everything you've got or else there's no point in playing. You just have to play the bigger game at the same time, that's all."

"What do you mean? What bigger game?"

"Well, let's say you're playing baseball, right? You want to win, right? You want to win more than anything in the world."

Tom nodded. That was the way he felt, no matter what Mrs. Lerner said. No matter what Mrs. Lerner said, he was always keeping score in his head, trying to win.

"So you play as hard as you can," Burt went on. "You practice. You get excellent. You work. You sweat. You play and try to win with everything you have in you."

"Right."

"But do you cheat?"

Tom laughed again. "No."

"Well, why not?" said Burt, giving his eleven-year-old little brother a friendly clap on the back of the head. "I thought you wanted to win more than anything in the world."

"I do."

"So why don't you cheat, if that's what it takes to win?"

Tom shrugged. "I don't know. 'Cause I don't want to be a cheater, that's why."

"Exactly. God didn't make you to be a cheater. He made you to be the most excellent Tom Harding–type guy in the universe. Being that guy he made you—that's the bigger game. So you play to win the game of baseball with everything you got, but if you lose . . ." He shrugged. "You feel bad for a while, but so what? Feelings are just feelings. The important thing is you keep working at being the excellent Tom Harding. Then even when you lose, even when you feel bad for a while, you can feel good, too, because you're still winning the bigger game."

They walked home the rest of the way in silence, as the light continued to die and the air turned a deeper blue and the first stars began to shine.

29.

Tom's eyes fluttered open. At first he saw nothing but a blurred darkness. Then the indigo evening world swam into focus. He saw the sky. He saw the charred timbers of the chapel ceiling. The blackened walls. He remembered.

The monastery. Dr. Cameron. He'd been shot. He was dying.

Already he didn't have the strength to move. He didn't even have the strength to breathe. He could almost feel his life draining out of him—just as his blood was draining out of him, spreading around him over the chapel floor.

He let his eyes fall closed. He lay still, waiting for the end. *At least it doesn't hurt,* he thought. He didn't even feel scared or sorry. He was just tired, that's all. He just wanted it all to end.

Dear God, he thought in a farewell prayer, *please comfort my mother. Please give her strength.*

A sunset wind moved over him. It felt refreshing on his face. He heard it whisper in the burned-out branches around him. In his fogged mind, it almost sounded like a voice.

With an effort he opened his eyes again. Was someone there with him in the dusk? Yes. Someone was standing above him, looking down at him. Tom squinted, trying to see through the gloom. Then he realized: no. It was just that painting on the wall. Those painted eyes with the line of blood trickling down beside them.

The eyes gazed at him with enormous sorrow and compassion. Tom tried to smile at them.

Bad day, he thought up at them. *It seems I've been murdered.*

Yes, the eyes responded at once. *That happens sometimes when you insist on telling the truth. People don't always appreciate it.*

Tom nodded slightly. He wondered whose voice that was.

Was it Burt's? It sounded a little like Burt. Maybe that's why there was blood on him. From where the sniper got him.

It's not so bad really, Tom told the eyes. *Maybe I'll get to see you in heaven.*

But when the eyes spoke again, the voice sounded more like Lisa's voice than Burt's.

The road to heaven isn't death, Tommy. It's life.

Tom peered up at the eyes through the darkness. His consciousness fading, he thought he saw the whole painting restored in its frame: Christ crucified, the rivulets of blood streaming down from under his crown of thorns.

But you *died,* Tom said to him. You *died and went to heaven.*

No, the eyes answered, sounding more like Burt again. *I lived. That's the whole point. I lived. And now you have to live, Tom.*

Tom did not think there was any energy left inside him, any strength with which he could feel anything. But at the words that came down to him from the painting on the wall, he felt something inside him tremble and break open. He felt something rush out of his center and spread through the rest of him, something dark and heavy that he had been keeping inside, keeping secret, secret even from himself, for a long time.

I can't live! he confessed to the painting. *That's the truth.*

I don't know how to live anymore! He gazed up desperately into the compassionate eyes and his whole soul cried out to them: *I don't know how to live! I'm so sad! I lost my brother! I've lost all my friends! I've lost my girl! My heart is broken! I don't care if I die! I want to die! I don't know how to live anymore!*

Tom thought the eyes would grow stern and angry now. He thought they would flash like lightning. What a horrible thing to think, after all. *I want to die.* What an awful thing.

But the eyes, gazing back at him with all his own pain inside them, said only, *Remember the Warrior. Play the bigger game.* Tom did not know whose voice this was anymore. Lisa's or Burt's or some other's or all of them together. *That's what I was trying to tell you,* it went on. *That's your mission. Live. And don't just live. Live in joy. Even in your sorrow, Tom, live in joy. That's what I made you for. Remember the Warrior. Play the bigger game.*

As he grew weaker, Tom's eyes sank shut again. But strangely, he felt relieved. He felt better. He had told the eyes the worst thing in his heart, and the eyes had not condemned him. Not at all. And really, he knew they were right. Deep down, he did want to live. Even with Burt gone, even with everything that had happened, he wanted to feel joy again. It was just that he was so weak, so tired . . .

Something touched his face. Something cold. Wet.

He's crying for me, Tom thought hazily.

But it was the rain. It had started again. It spilled down lightly out of the evening sky through the chapel roof and washed over his cheeks, refreshing him a little, giving him a little strength.

Maybe I can still do something, he thought. *Maybe I can reach my phone, anyway. Maybe I can call for help.*

He felt awfully bad, awfully tired. But he might be able to do that. Just get his phone out of his pocket. Just dial 911. *That couldn't be so hard*, he thought.

He was wrong, though. It was hard. It was fantastically, amazingly, unbelievably hard. Moving his arm even a little bit required an effort of will greater than any he had ever made. He had to focus every bit of his energy on getting his hand to lift off the floor. Using all his strength, he lifted it—lifted it—then dropped it onto his waist. Now, slowly, slowly, he began to push the hand down toward his pants pocket. The work made him cough weakly. He felt the blood boil and gurgle in his chest. He thought for sure he would collapse and die before he managed actually to reach into the pocket, to get a grip on the edge of his phone. But he did it. He caught the slippery little rectangle of plastic between the tips of his fingers. He began to draw the phone out—and then he lost his hold on it. It slipped from his grasp.

He let out a noise of frustration. He gazed up into the

eyes watching him. The rain pattered down on him gently. He gathered his strength again and willed his hand back down into his pocket. He willed his fingers to pincer the phone again. To work the phone—slowly, ever so slowly—out onto his belt buckle . . .

He had to rest a moment after that. He lay on the floor in the pool of his own blood, gasping and coughing. The eyes watched him sorrowfully from the frame on the wall.

I know, I know, he told them. *My mission. Right. Live.*

He went back to work. He willed his hand to his phone again. He picked it up off his shirtfront. He lifted it until he could see it there in his hand. He pressed the numbers for the police: 9 . . . 1 . . . 1 . . .

And the readout said: *No service.*

Tom lost what little breath he had and his hand fell back onto his belly, the phone still grasped in his fingers.

No service.

Sure, of course. He was in the middle of the woods. No cell tower nearby. Trees all around him. The chapel walls around him. No way to get a signal here unless he . . .

Tom nearly laughed in despair at the thought. Yes, he might get a signal if he could move out of the chapel, if he could make it out to that jutting ledge of rock at the edge of the monastery, that natural balcony overlooking the town below. He might get a signal out on the ledge, but how was he supposed to get there? Fly? He could barely move his hand to his pocket.

He cast an appeal at the eyes looking down on him. The eyes were silent now. It didn't matter. He didn't need the eyes to tell him what he had to do. He already knew. He had to try.

He gathered himself for the attempt. If moving his hand had been hard, how much harder was it going to be to get his whole body moving? Another moment of focus, and then, grunting with the explosive effort, he rolled onto his stomach, blood spilling over his lips as he coughed and gasped for air.

He managed to lift his head, to lift his eyes and look out ahead of him. It was hard to see. Harder than ever. It was getting darker. And he was fading. And there was something else, too. What was that? Tom squinted. Stared.

Fog. Yes. Thick fog just beyond the edge of the chapel. The marine layer seemed to have moved in as he was lying there. The cottony white mass had pushed up across the mountain, swallowing the stunted, fire-charred trees until they were nothing but twisted black figures in the depths of the mist. It seemed to Tom the fog was full of such figures, and that they were almost more like hunched, hulking human shapes than like trees. It seemed to him these creatures hunkered in the depths of the fog were waiting for him to come toward them, pacing like zombies and waiting until they could get their claws on him and devour him. And the look of them, their eyes. They were so . . . so . . .

. . . *malevolent*, he thought.

He shook his head trying to clear it, but the fog—and the creatures hulking in the fog—remained. Sweat poured down into his eyes, making them sting. The rain made his hair feel heavy and damp.

He was losing strength fast. If he was going to move, he had to move now. Whatever was in that fog—trees or creatures—whatever—he was going to have to face them, get past them, get to that balcony of rock.

He started crawling. Well, *crawling* was too nice a word for it. Clutching his phone in his hand, he started dragging himself over the chapel floor, elbow and knee forward—drag—the other elbow and knee forward—drag. The effort made him cough again. The cough brought more blood up into his mouth. The blood spilled out, dripping down his chin.

He dragged himself elbow over elbow, inch by inch, toward the edge of the chapel floor. He tumbled off the edge into the dirt, and even though it was hardly any distance at all, he felt like he had fallen off a ten-story building. The landing jolted him and made him cough again. He spit blood, staining the earth.

He rolled over onto his back, exhausted. The rain fell onto his face. The blood gurgled in his throat so that he thought he would strangle on it. With a groan, he rolled over onto his belly again and kept dragging himself through the dirt—right into the fog.

But a strange thing happened now. The fog began to dissolve around him. With every yard of ground Tom crawled, a yard of fog dissipated into a mere drizzle, and the front of the marine layer seemed to recede. The creatures inside the fog fell back with it. Where they had stood, the twisted trees began to appear more clearly on every side of him. Still hanging on to his phone, Tom dragged himself another yard and another, and the mist and its malevolent creatures continued to dissolve around him, the main body of the fog and the things within continued to fall back like an army in retreat. There was the shelf of rock up ahead, now visible as the fog vanished. There were the lights of the town sparkling through the mist in the gathering night below. It took every ounce of his failing will and failing strength to shift his arm and leg forward one more time, to dig his elbow into the ground and brace his knee against the surface and push and push and push himself forward another few inches, another half a foot, but he did it, and then he started the process all over again. The sweat and rain mingled on his forehead. The breath wheezed and whistled in his closing throat. He thought of nothing, focused on nothing but moving his body through the dirt, beneath the blackened trees, and through the light, cold rain that fell on him as the fog dissolved.

Now—to his astonishment—his hand touched the cold rock. He saw the white of it beneath his face. He lifted his eyes and saw the cliff. There was no more fog at all, no more trees over him or in front of him. There was nothing but the open sky. His phone was still gripped in his sweaty, dirty hand. He brought it slowly up in front of his face.

No service.

The same message on the readout as before. No signal at all.

But then the message winked out. In its place, there was a bar, a single bar. He had a signal. A low signal. But maybe it was enough.

He coughed blood. He moved his shaky thumb over the dial pad. It hovered over the Redial button.

Don't make a mistake, he thought. *You won't get another chance.*

He brought his thumb down hard. He heard the tones playing through the speaker.

One bar, he thought. *It has to be enough.*

It was. Far away, he heard the phone ringing. He willed himself to lift the phone to his ear.

"Nine-one-one," a woman's voice said. "What's your emergency?"

Tom opened his mouth to answer—and nothing came out but blood. He didn't have the breath to form the words.

"Hello?" said the operator. "Is anyone there? What's your emergency?"

Tom forced himself to speak.

"The monastery."

"What? What? Hello?"

"The Santa Maria Monastery," whispered Tom. "I've been shot. I'm dying. Help me."

His hand and face fell to the rock together and he lost consciousness.

PART IV

THE RETURN OF THE LYING MAN

30.

The garden was dark now. The people were gone. The white temples, the green lawns, the vivid flower gardens—all the colors seemed somehow to have drained out of them. They were all draped in shadow. They looked like the abandoned scenery of a stage set, covered in canvas after the show has ended.

Tom stood at the edge of the place he had thought was heaven. He lingered there as the twilight fell. As the scene grew darker around him, he saw that a new scene began to come into view beyond the garden's far border. A light began breaking through the distant gloaming, a white radiance rising like the dawn. It seemed as if the garden had somehow blocked this light from his vision before and that now, as the temples and the paths and flowers faded, the hidden brilliance was revealed.

The light grew brighter as the garden shaded over into nothingness—brighter and brighter until Tom could barely look at it directly. Holding up his hand to shield his eyes, he squinted into the whiteness. *There's something in there*, he thought. There were shapes dimly visible, rising and falling in a jagged skyline. A whole city, it seemed, was hidden in this radiance, vast and majestic towers and palaces rising obscurely in the depths of the light.

As Tom stood staring, trying to make out the details of the scene, a figure—a man—emerged from the glare and came toward him. He stepped to the edge of the visible and stopped. He was just a small shape against the bright skyline. But Tom knew him. Tom would have known him anywhere.

His heart in his throat, his eyes filling, Tom stood and gazed at the man across the vast space between them, the uncrossable space. He ached to go to him and see his face and hear his voice. But this was not that time.

The figure seemed to gaze back at him as the rising light

began to engulf him. Then, very slowly, he lifted his right arm and set his hand against his forehead in a crisp military salute.

A single tear overflowed Tom's eye and ran down his cheek. The distant light grew brighter and brighter. It was soon so bright that the saluting figure was obscured by its glare. And yet the light grew brighter still until finally it overcame the man completely. He seemed to vanish into it.

And there was nothing but the light.

———

With that, Tom opened his eyes and saw his mother. She was sleeping in a chair beside his hospital bed. She was leaning far forward, resting her head on her arms, resting her arms on the edge of his mattress.

Tom lifted his hand and touched her hair gently.

The gesture woke her at once. She raised her face, confused at first. She looked around for a moment and then seemed to remember where she was. Then she saw him.

"Tom?" she said, her voice breaking. "Tom!"

His mouth moved as he tried to whisper an answer.

Frantic, his mother reached for the plastic tube that hung beside his bed—the tube that held the Call button that would summon a nurse. The tube slipped through her trembling fingers twice before she could get ahold of it. Then she got it, pressed the button quickly—and let it drop.

She seized hold of Tom's hand with both her hands. She brought his hand to her face and started kissing it again and again. She was weeping.

Tom's eyes fluttered shut again. He did not have the strength to keep them open. His mother pressed his hand against her cheek and he felt her tears on the back of it. He heard her sobbing his name again and again.

His eyes closed, he smiled. He didn't remember everything that happened, but he had a sure and certain understanding that he had found his way. Through the fog, through his memory, through his sorrow, out of his coma, back to his life.

And he was going to live.

31.

The next time Tom woke, it was night and he was alone. At first, a thrill of fear went through him. He wasn't sure why. *What are you afraid of?* he asked himself. In answer, images flashed through his mind: empty rooms, fog-shrouded streets, hunkering, malevolent zombies with their outstretched claws . . .

Like something out of a horror movie. He couldn't make sense of it. *I must've had a bad dream*, he thought.

He looked around him. He was in a hospital room just as he had been before. His mother was gone now and the lights were out. The room was dark. As his eyes adjusted, Tom could see there was a TV hanging on the wall in front of him. There was a window on the wall to his left. Under the window was a small, low table with a vase of carnations on it.

How had he gotten here? He looked down at himself. There were cords and tubes running in and out of him. There was a contraption attached to his index finger that ran to a machine on the nightstand beside his bed. The numbers on the machine glowed with a red light, showing his pulse rate. Standing beside the nightstand was a pole with a bag of fluid hanging on it. A tube ran out of the bag and down to a gauze bandage on his arm. Tom had been in the hospital once before when he'd had appendicitis, and he knew that under the bandage there was an unpleasantly large needle embedded in his flesh, carrying the fluid into his vein. As he continued to examine himself, he saw that his upper body was wrapped in bandages beneath his pajamas. He'd clearly been injured pretty badly.

He turned his head. On the opposite side of the room from the window, there was another bed. It was empty now, but there had been a man in it before, a lanky young man with long blond hair. Tom wasn't sure how he knew this, but he knew the man had cut his wrists for some reason, trying to kill himself. The young man had lingered for a while in a coma, but he hadn't made it through. He was gone.

Tom looked up at the ceiling. He tried to remember what had happened to him. There had been pain. Fog. Those weird monsters . . .

No, that couldn't be right. That didn't make sense. A dream.

Well, he was sure to find out the truth eventually. Finding out the truth was a habit with him—more of an obsession, really. The important thing for right now was that he was getting better. He could feel it. Weak as he was, he could feel the strength beginning to return to him. Soon he'd be on his feet again, back in his ordinary life. Life had been pretty rough these last six months, since Burt had died. But he thought maybe now it would start to get better. He would always miss Burt. But Burt was okay. Burt was good. He wasn't sure how he knew that either, but he did.

And for himself, after all the grief he'd felt, he knew now there'd be good times, too. He looked forward to being back in school. He could imagine himself sitting at his desk in the *Sentinel*'s office again, joking around with Lisa. He could see Lisa's pale, freckled face framed by the tumbling red hair, the bright green eyes behind the round glasses. He smiled to himself, lying in the dark. He'd never actually realized until now how much he liked her—really liked her. And she liked him, too, didn't she? Funny, that had never occurred to him before. It was probably because he'd wasted too much time pining for . . .

Marie.

He stopped smiling.

Marie. Yes. All at once, he remembered. Marie flirting with him at school. Kissing him outside her house. Smiling at him at the dining room table as her father toasted him with an orange juice glass while the rainbows from the chandelier prisms danced around them. And then . . . and then Marie and Gordon in the gym and the things she had said when she didn't know Tom was listening. And then Dr. Cameron . . .

The rest came back to him in one sudden rush.

You'll be pulling a thread that will unravel relationships throughout this town, throughout this state, even beyond that.

The burned-out monastery amid the blackened trees. Dr. Cameron standing at the chapel entrance, the gun in his hand.

This is what happens to people who can't keep their mouths shut.

The gunshot.

Tom opened his mouth, breathing hard. The memories fell into place like playing cards riffled by an invisible hand. Dr. Cameron had tried to murder him because he'd found out that he was the one selling drugs to the football team. His debt; his borrowing; his drug dealing; his gambling—the whole deal. He had the evidence—Karen Lee's story—recorded on his phone.

He realized he had to tell someone right away. He had to make the story public fast in order to protect Karen Lee from Dr. Cameron's retribution. And he had to tell the police as well.

He remembered his mother reaching for the Call button by his bed—to summon the nurse. That's what he had to do. Summon the nurse. Have her call his mom. Lisa. The cops.

Fully awake now finally, he gingerly turned around on the mattress. He saw the tube with the Call button dangling from a cord on the wall. His chest ached as he reached across himself with his free arm—the arm without the needle in it—as he reached for the button.

But just then, the door swung open. A man stood in the doorway. His figure was silhouetted by the light from the hall, but Tom could see he was wearing the blue scrubs of a doctor. The man stepped forward and the door swung shut, covering the man in shadow.

Tom's fingers closed around the Call button tube—but the very next moment, the tube was pulled from his fingers. The man in scrubs was standing directly over him.

"You never should have come back, Tom," he said. "You should have stayed in the monastery. You should have stayed dead."

Tom recognized the voice immediately: it was the Lying Man.

32.

The red-light numbers on the pulse monitor rose rapidly as Tom's heart began to pound in his aching chest. The Lying Man looked down at him from what seemed a great height.

"Believe me, your death is the best thing for everyone," he said in his calm, hypnotic, soothing voice. "You had no business coming back."

Tom remembered everything in that moment. The

empty house. The fog in the streets. The malevolents reaching for him with their long claws, trying to tear him apart. It wasn't a dream. It wasn't a dream at all. It was real.

And the Lying Man was real. The King of Death had come back to claim him. Tom peered up through the darkness until the Lying Man's face became clear above him: Dr. Cameron.

"I didn't want to take this risk," he told Tom serenely. "I hoped you'd have the good sense to die when you were supposed to. I thought you *were* dead when I left you at the monastery. But you just don't know when to quit, Tom. So I'll have to help you. This won't take long. And the way I do it, it won't even leave a trace. After all, I'm a doctor. And I'll tell them: your lungs just couldn't heal . . ."

Tom tried to shout for help, but his voice was too weak—and Dr. Cameron was way too fast. The big man moved like a panther. He yanked the pillow out from under Tom's head—and in the same motion, in the same second— brought it down over Tom's face.

The doctor was strong—and Tom had no strength in him at all. The pillow pressed down, pinning him to the bed. It closed off his nose and mouth, cut off his air completely. He felt his lungs working helplessly in his aching chest. He couldn't draw breath. He was suffocating.

He tried to fight, to get out from under, but it was no

use. He reached up and tried to push Dr. Cameron's hands away, but the man's arms were immensely powerful, locked into position, like stone pillars, unmovable. With every second Tom tried to push them away, he lost strength. A dizziness began to swim around him. He felt he was sinking into unconsciousness. He knew that this time he would never return.

He stopped fighting, stopped trying to push at Cameron's hands. Instead, he dropped his arms, reached across himself. Felt for the bandage on the inside of his elbow. As the airless heat beneath the pillow closed over him like a sprung trap, as his consciousness began to swim and spin away, he tore the bandage off his own skin. Felt for the end of the tube, for the needle embedded in his flesh.

He ripped the needle out of himself and blindly plunged it into Cameron's body.

Through the muffling pillow, Tom heard the doctor cry out in pain. He felt the man's hold on the pillow loosen. With all the strength he had, Tom twisted his body away from him, out from under the pillow. He rolled over onto his side, taking a great, welcome gasp of air.

And then he slid off the edge of the bed and tumbled to the floor.

It was a long drop, and he hit hard. He took the jolt on his shoulder, but he felt it in his chest, a jarring, rattling pain.

He coughed, trying to catch his breath. The room filled with a high-pitched alarm as the heart monitor wire was torn off his finger and the monitor flatlined, its red numbers dropping to zero as if Tom had died.

Tom had not died. Not yet. But now Dr. Cameron cursed and came at him once again.

Tom caught a glimpse of the man striding around the bed, charging through the shadows. The heart monitor continued its high-pitched scream, and Tom wished he had the breath to echo it.

Dr. Cameron swiftly turned the corner of the bed. Tom rolled over again. He hit the table under the window. Ignoring the pain in his chest, he reached up and grabbed the table's edge. He pulled himself up on it and reached for the flower vase with his free hand.

Dr. Cameron grabbed him, his fingers digging into his shoulder. Tom was shocked at the power of the man's grip. Dr. Cameron started to force him down to the floor.

Tom wrapped his hand around the flower vase and brought it crashing into the side of Dr. Cameron's head.

Dr. Cameron shouted as the vase shattered, as the broken edge of it sliced into his cheek. Blinded and in pain, he reared back, rose up, clutching at his own eyes.

At the same moment, the door of the room opened. A nurse came rushing in, flipping on the light.

She had heard the alarm—the heart monitor. She had seen the readout at the nursing station down the hall. She had seen the numbers drop. She'd come rushing in to make sure Tom was all right. As the room was flooded with light, she saw Dr. Cameron staggering backward, clutching at his bleeding face.

"Doctor?" she said. "Are you all right?"

Over the endless scream of the monitor's alarm, Tom heard Dr. Cameron shout, "Get out of my way!" Propped against the table, he saw the bleeding doctor stumble toward the nurse and shove her aside as he headed for the door.

Coughing, Tom slid down to the floor. He stared up at the ceiling. He heard Dr. Cameron's footsteps running away down the hall. And yet he thought he could still hear him nearby, speaking into his ear.

No, it wasn't Dr. Cameron. It was the Lying Man.

You just don't know when to quit, Tom, he said.

Tom closed his eyes and smiled weakly. "I'll never quit," he whispered.

EPILOGUE: WHEN IT WAS OVER

I t was all the same," said Tom, "but it was all different."

He was in the living room of his house. He was sitting in the easy chair, a blanket over his legs. His mother and Lisa were sitting on the sofa across from him, directly beneath the wall of windows. Tom had been home from the hospital only a week. He still didn't have a lot of strength. He could barely walk a few steps before he had to rest again.

He pointed at the windows. "That's where the malevolents came through. They broke right through the glass. I ran past them to the stairs and got into my room. But the Lying Man talked me into leaving and then they got me. That was the second time my heart stopped. After that, Lisa came and we figured out together what was going on."

"Glad I could help," said Lisa with a quirky smile.

"What a strange dream," said Tom's mother.

"I don't think it was a dream," Tom told her. "Not exactly. I think it was all true somehow. It was just . . . I was just seeing it with my imagination, you know?"

Tom's mom made a puzzled face, but Lisa said, "No, I get that. I believe that. Just because something happens in your imagination, that doesn't mean it's imaginary."

Tom let out a startled laugh. "That's just what you said when you came to the house. Almost those exact words. It was really helpful."

"Really?" said Lisa. She preened herself comically, fluffing her hair, trying to hide the fact that she really was pleased. "That just shows you how wise I am even when I'm only in your mind."

"You know, it does actually," Tom said to her—and the way he said it made Lisa blush, which, in turn, gave Tom a great deal of pleasure.

"Personally," Tom's mother chimed in, "I find the real world dangerous enough without having to imagine anything. I really don't know what I would have done if I had lost you . . ." Those last words were muffled in tears. She raised her hand to her overflowing eyes.

Lisa reached out and touched her arm. "Don't worry," she said. "Tom would never die when there was still a good story to tell."

Tom laughed and coughed. "It was a good story, all right. It was a great story."

It was. The fall of Dr. Cameron had been fast and hard. If anyone—any of the doctor's friends on the police force or in the government—had been thinking of helping him or trying to cover up for him, they thought better of it when Tom's follow-up story explaining who had supplied drugs to the Tigers hit first the *Sentinel*, and then—as Lisa's bluff became reality—the front page of *USA Today*. Next, the big news sites on the Web had picked it up: "School Paper Busts Drug-Dealing Doc." There had even been a couple of TV stories about it. Fox News and CNN had both interviewed Lisa, and both wanted to interview Tom when he was well enough. Given the publicity—and given Karen Lee's testimony and the testimony from some of the Tigers players—and given Tom's testimony about being shot and assaulted in his hospital room, Dr. Cameron had been charged with attempted murder and various counts of drug dealing. If he was convicted, he could go to prison for life. Coach Petrie was now under investigation as well. And rumor had it that the investigation was starting to spread out to others who had received drugs from the doctor, people with organized-crime connections that went beyond the state line.

There was no telling where it would end. It was a great story. And it had all started with Tom.

Tom's mother's eyes still glistened with tears, but she smiled. "It's amazing," she said. "I raised two heroes. Burt would risk everything to protect people, and Tom would risk everything to get to the truth."

"Well," Tom said, "the truth will set you free, right?"

"Oh, I don't know," Lisa said with a laugh. "I don't think it's going to work out that way for Dr. Cameron."

Tom's mother got up from the sofa and came toward him. "I'm proud of both my boys," she said, "but I'll tell you, Lisa: having hero sons is not easy on a mom. Not easy at all."

She came to where Tom sat and adjusted the blanket on his legs. She had put a mug full of chicken soup on the table beside him. She lifted it now and put it into his hands.

"Drink some of this," she said, her eyes still wet and glistening. "You need to build up your strength."

As Tom took the mug, he looked past his mother at Lisa. He rolled his eyes secretly and she lifted her shoulders in an amiable shrug. The truth was: Tom hated chicken soup. He hated having a blanket on his legs as if he were an old man. He wasn't even cold. And he wasn't particularly hungry either. He didn't really want his mother fussing over him and worrying about him all the time.

But he lifted his cheek to her as she leaned down to kiss him. He said, "Thanks, Mom." And he drank the soup.

There were some truths he would never tell.

READING GROUP GUIDE

1. Have you ever found yourself in a situation where
   nothing felt right: people close to you seemed to be
   missing, nothing seemed "normal"? How did you
   respond? What did you think was happening?
2. Tom feels like he's won the lottery now that Marie
   seems to be interested in him—and he wants to believe
   everything she tells him. Do you think he was too
   trusting of her? Would you have been?
3. One of the things Tom holds on to in the story is that
   Burt never lied. Is there anyone in your life that you
   have that kind of confidence in? How does it affect your
   relationship to have that kind of trust?
4. "Because as long as you do what's right, you won't mind
   if everyone knows." Even though Tom knows this is
   true, is it difficult to do this? What's the right thing to
   do when you do mess up?

5. At one point Tom realizes, "whatever the truth turns out to be, it's better to know than not to know. There's no other way to live." Do you believe that? Or do you ascribe more to the belief that ignorance is bliss? When has the truth been incredibly hard for you to hear? Were you ultimately glad you knew?

6. Karen Lee had known for a while that Dr. Cameron was providing illegal drugs to the football team but she was afraid to do anything about it. How difficult is it to stand up for the truth when you know there could be very real consequences such as the loss of a job or danger to yourself? Have you ever been in a situation like that?

7. Burt tells Tom, "Being the guy he made you—that's the bigger game." How do you play the bigger game in your life? What were you made to do?

8. Tom was so focused on Marie that he didn't realize how much Lisa really cared about him. Have you ever missed out—or almost missed out—on something good because it wasn't what you thought you wanted?

9. At the monastery Tom hears a voice tell him: "That's your mission. Live. And don't just live. Live in joy. Even in your sorrow, Tom, live in joy. That's what I made you for. Remember the Warrior. Play the bigger game." If you had been in Tom's place, shot and dying in the monastery, would you have continued to fight? What would you have hung on to that was worth fighting—and living—for?

THE MINDWAR TRILOGY

A COMPLEX THRILLER ABOUT A SEEMINGLY ORDINARY
TEENAGER WHO DISCOVERS A HIDDEN GIFT—A GIFT THAT
COULD MAKE HIM A HERO . . . OR COST HIM EVERYTHING.

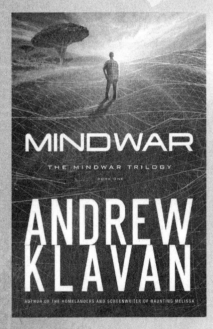

AVAILABLE IN PRINT AND E-BOOK

AVAILABLE IN PRINT AND E-BOOK
MARCH 2015

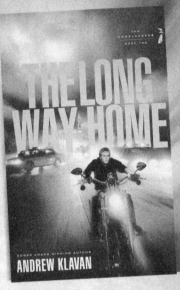

DO RIGHT.
FEAR NOTHING.

ANDREW KLAVAN
EDGAR AWARD-WINNING AUTHOR

CRAZY
DANGEROUS

DO RIGHT. FEAR NOTHING

AVAILABLE IN PRINT AND E-BOOK

ABOUT THE AUTHOR

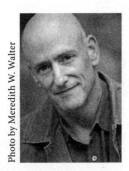

Photo by Meredith W. Walter

Andrew Klavan is a bestselling, award-winning thriller novelist whose books have been made into major motion pictures. He broke into the YA scene with the bestselling Homelanders series, starting with *The Last Thing I Remember*. He is also a screenwriter and scripted the innovative movie-in-an-app *Haunting Melissa*.